PRAISE FOR THE SERIES

EDITOR'S PICK: *"A riveting debut that blends post-apocalyptic adventure with conspiracy-based sci-fi thriller... Eliason's energetic pacing, entertaining characters, and crisp world-building create smart, satisfying reading. A promising start to a series."*

—PUBLISHER'S WEEKLY BOOKLIFE

"Wonderfully staggering revelations all the way to the cliffhanger ending...(a) thoroughly absorbing post-apocalyptic tale."

—KIRKUS REVIEWS

THE BIRTH OF PARADISE

THE BIRTH OF PARADISE

A MERU INITIATIVE NOVELLA

NATHANIEL ELIASON

Heart Mind

THE BIRTH OF PARADISE
A Meru Initiative Novella

FIRST EDITION

ISBN   978-1-5445-5059-6   *Hardcover*
       978-1-5445-5058-9   *Paperback*
       978-1-5445-5060-2   *Ebook*
       978-1-5445-5067-1   *Audiobook*

FOR COSETTE, SUTTON, KAIA, AND ARDEN

CONTENTS

THE WORLD OF MERU

For updates on the next book in the Meru Initiative, be sure to join the mailing list at www.meruinitiative.com.

PROLOGUE

BE CAREFUL.

If Felix finds you reading this, I can only imagine what might happen to you. But read it you must because whoever entrusted it to you believes you're ready to understand what happened on the day death ended. What really happened.

I'm deeply ashamed by what I've done. If I had been strong enough to accept my mortality, I might not have been so gullible. And if I hadn't been so eager to see Felix's dream come to life, so willing to massage the story of that day, then you might not be reading this in the situation you are in.

I've done my best to catalog everything about the fall, about the Meru Initiative, and this will be my last entry. Unlike the other documents, it's more of a story than a historical record, but I believe it is important to hear so you know what it was like on that fateful day. So you can hear, in Felix's words, how he sold me on this paradise and, through my transformation from dubious skeptic to true believer, how I convinced the world.

I am long gone from the Meru you inhabit, so I am safe. But you aren't. Not yet. Perhaps once you read this, you'll wish to escape, too, in which case the only guidance I can give you is to look for us. Felix will find this eventually, so I cannot give too many details for our own protection. But if you were smart enough to get this far, you'll be smart enough to take the next step too.

Please forgive me.

ROHAN PATEL

CHAPTER 1

THE CALL CAME AS I LEFT AN INTERVIEW WITH THE CEO of a robotics company. He'd developed appendages with the dexterity to pick strawberries better than a human could, one of the remaining great challenges for robotics, and was under fire for his implicit promise to put the last farm laborers out of a job.

It was the perfect story for what had become my niche. Bold, forward-thinking technologists dragging the world kicking and screaming into the future. I'd spent years cultivating this beat, building relationships, honing my craft. I wasn't content to be another journalist with a microphone; I wanted to be the voice that could make or break reputations, the person who separated genuine visionaries from charlatans.

A guard handed me my phone as I stepped out into the hazy Los Angeles heat. The moment the device touched my palm, it rang with a call from an unknown number.

I never answered unknown calls. But something compelled me to pick up that call on that day.

"Hello?"

"Hello! Rohan?"

His eagerness sang through the phone as though he was about to sell me something, but I decided to entertain him for a moment longer. "Speaking. Who is this?"

"This is Felix. Felix Craft. I have a proposition for you."

Disbelief struck first.

Felix Craft was arguably the most famous businessman in the world and had been my white whale for years. In high school and throughout college, I'd watched countless hours of his interviews and product demos. I'd even mimicked his gestures as he strode across the stage, with his tweed blazer and slicked-back hair, breathlessly introducing some new game or piece of hardware.

As hard as it was to believe, I'd have known his voice anywhere. This was him. After six years of silence, after the scandal, after everyone wrote him off as another tragic genius who'd lost his mind, he was calling me. I had to tamp down my excitement. Whether he'd finally cracked consciousness transfer or gone completely mad trying, either story could make my career.

"Are you there, Rohan?"

"I—er—yes. Sorry. I'm just..."

Felix laughed his trademark cackle, reinforcing my confidence further. "You didn't truly believe I was gone, did you?"

The truth was, I did. After he was kicked out of his company, Imgen, hardly anyone had heard from him. The only person who claimed to have seen him was his old business partner, Vance Banner, and he said Felix had lost his mind. Though that wasn't saying much, given Vance's own decline.

"No one's heard from you. I'm sorry. I'm having a hard time processing this. Why are you calling *me*?"

"Don't be so modest, Rohan. Everyone in the valley knows who you are."

The compliment landed exactly where he intended, and I had to resist being too flustered by it.

"Don't you live in Texas?"

"The *metaphorical* valley. Sure, you're not a household name, but the household names are entertainers. They look at new technology and just go 'Wowza.' You know how to ask the right questions. You know how to interrogate these grand advances in engineering and technology."

"Are you asking me to interview you?"

"Much more than that." He paused and took a breath so deep I could hear the air over the microphone. "I'm extending you an invitation. I want you to join me for the most important day in the history of man's relationship with machines."

I'd heard him use that line at least five times in prior speeches. But if this was what I thought it was, he might be telling the truth for once.

Before I could respond, he continued. "I've done it, Rohan. It's been a long and painful road to get here, but I'm quite certain I've solved it this time." Then he took another deep breath, one I knew was purely to heighten the drama. "Will you join me for the birth of paradise?"

※ ※ ※

Before he hung up, he told me there would be a jet waiting for me at Van Nuys in two days. Part of me knew there might be ulterior motives I wasn't seeing. But this was Felix Craft. The story I'd been chasing my entire career was offering itself to me on a silver platter. If Felix had succeeded, I'd be the reporter who broke the biggest technological achievement in human history. If he'd failed, I'd finally have the definitive story of his downfall.

I didn't have much to pack or prepare. I was living out of two suitcases at the time: one for my personal things and the other for my recording gear, with no partner or even pets to coordinate with. So I spent the two days hopping between coffee shops, restaurants, and bars, doing research and preparing my notes.

I found little new information, but that didn't matter. I knew Felix's history better than I knew my parents'—every triumph, every failure, every controversy. I'd been building toward this moment for years, collecting every scrap of information about his consciousness transfer project. I brushed up on my philosophy of mind, a favorite topic of his, and reread the last reports from before that awful accident. Then I spent hours crafting my interview strategy.

I mapped out two narratives: one for his victory and one for his madness. Either way, I'd need to push past his famous charm and deflections. The consensus was that his wife's death had driven him to pursue the impossible, like Newton's alchemy or Tesla's global wireless power. But consensus had been wrong before. Especially about Felix.

Cedar pollen and dust hit my lungs the moment the plane door opened in Dallas, the dry Texas air carrying the scent of scorched grass. I'd woken up with a cough, likely the consequences of so much travel and poor sleep, and I had to pause to catch my breath, heaving into my arm before descending the stairs.

The autocab slowed as it passed through the towering wrought-metal gate that guarded his driveway, the doors swinging in automatically, each attached to a column of stone with golden phoenixes perched atop. The phoenix had long been Felix's spirit animal of sorts, his mythical fascination. Many assumed that the feather wrapped along the bottom of the Imgen logo was from a hawk or eagle or other predator, but from the beginning, Felix was obsessed with the mysteries of life and death, birth and rebirth.

It might seem odd that someone so driven by technology could be enraptured with the mythical. But it fit with Felix's hubris. You must believe in God to become a god. And Felix believed in much more than just God.

The driveway was flanked by oaks and terminated in a round-about encircling a great pond. Submerged fountains formed arcs across the lily pads, and ripples hid the koi below. He was a man of technology, one who had committed his life to harnessing the forces of electricity and silicon to change the world. Yet in his private life, he seemed to want to escape the changes he'd manifested. Everywhere I looked, his home elevated the ancient. A reminder that the things we created and surrounded ourselves with could outlive us if built with care.

As the car stopped, he appeared atop his sweeping marble stairs, beaming at me. Something about the glint in his eyes told me this would be the most important day in both our lives.

CHAPTER 2

MY FIRST IMPRESSION AS I STEPPED OUT OF THE CAR was that Felix had transformed. The sunken eyes and gray pallor from the last photos of him had vanished. His hair was white, but vibrant. He looked as though he'd barely aged in the ten years since he was fired. Perhaps he'd even aged backward, as someone his age occasionally appeared to do when they rediscovered the spark of life.

As I ascended the stairs, an android stepped between us, its arm outstretched. It moved with the smoothness of a human, no typical robotic jerkiness or hesitation, as if Felix had tinkered with it himself to make it more delicate than its industrial or military counterparts. It was short, perhaps designed that way, to appear less intimidating, and a faint blue glow emitted from the joints as well as around the blank white faceplate.

"Just a formality," Felix said, his tone reassuring.

I nodded, and the android extended an arm, a small medical scanner in its hand. Imgen had designed these after the last pandemic, a way to quickly check someone for viral or bacterial infections.

The blue light swept over me once, then again. The android paused, its head tilting slightly. It adjusted something on the scanner and repeated the process, this time slowly, methodically. The light lingered at my chest, my throat.

"Is everything all right?" I asked, leaning around its shoulder to try to glimpse the screen.

Felix watched, his eyes fixed not on me but on the device. "Just being thorough."

"Surprised you're worried about getting sick," I said, trying to break the strange tension.

"I'm not," Felix replied, his gaze still on the scanner. "But Susan insisted I play it safe. Just in case."

I stifled a cough as the android lowered the device and retreated to Felix, showing him the readout. Felix studied it, his lips moving slightly as if reading something important. Then his face broke into a satisfied smile.

"Very good. Very good." He looked at me with an expression I couldn't quite read. "Everything's exactly as it should be." Then he descended the steps to me and grabbed my hand in both of his with surprising strength. "Rohan, I'm so honored you could be here for this."

"The pleasure is all mine, Dr. Craft."

"Please. Felix."

There was something disarming about his casualness. As though I'd known him much longer than I had. "Very well then, Felix."

"Come in. Come in," he said as he released my hand and gestured toward the door.

"Should I bring my equipment?"

"It will all be handled. I can assure you my friends will treat it with the utmost care."

As if on cue, another pair of androids emerged through the door and began descending the stairs toward the car.

The rotunda stopped me cold. A crystal chandelier nearly

touched the paw foot table below. Sweeping staircases curled to the landing above. Each step revealed new art. A few familiar pieces lined the walls, and a massive renaissance crucifixion dominated the top of the stairs. Between the paintings, sculptures sat in recessed alcoves.

As I scanned the artwork, one piece stood out. "Is that—"

"The Shiva Nataraja? Yes. Yes, it is."

I huffed a laugh. "So the rumors were true."

"I tried very hard to keep that purchase secret."

"I've long dreamed of seeing it in person."

"You can touch it if you like."

"I'm quite satisfied being in its presence." I crossed the hall to study the dancing god enclosed in a flaming halo, holding in his hands the means of universal creation and destruction.

Felix stood behind me, his breath slow and contemplative. Although he saw the statue every day, it clearly hadn't lost its impact on him.

We lingered in silence as my eyes drifted around the other statues and decorations in the room. As I inspected the chandelier, I realized the rings supporting the crystals were not merely golden bands but delicately carved ouroboros.

"It's a beautiful collection."

"And I sense you've recognized the theme."

I nodded. "Death and rebirth, the eternal circle of life, creation and destruction."

"Eternal…" A mischievous smile crept across Felix's lips as he said it. "Perhaps not if I have my way."

"Shiva might be disappointed you're stealing his thunder."

"Well, you know the gods, always quarreling and fighting with one another."

"And you among them?"

The smile returned. "A man can dream, can't he?" Then he

turned to load me into the house. "Come along. Come along. Your listeners aren't tuning in to hear us quibble about religion, as engrossing as I suspect that would be for the two of us."

I followed him as we passed beneath the stairs, entering a hallway flanked by trees and photos from his early days at Imgen. "On the contrary. This is exactly the kind of thing my audience enjoys. You of all people appreciate the value in setting the stage."

"Indeed I do. Perhaps I'm simply eager."

"I don't blame you," I said as we crossed into the living room. A U-shaped couch faced the hills beyond through floor-to-ceiling windows. It was a stark contrast to the more traditional design of the front of the house, but the justification hit me in a flash. The wall of glass was not so much a statement as an attempt to blend the house into its environment while still protecting it from the brutal heat.

"Can I get you anything?" Felix asked as he continued into the kitchen.

"A cortado would be lovely."

"Certainly," he said and nodded to some unseen camera. A moment later, the familiar hiss of steam echoed from the room. Then the androids from outside reentered, carrying my boxes of equipment between them.

"If you're comfortable entrusting them to the setup, we could continue the tour. I assume you have instructions?"

"Yes. One moment." I fished out my phone and found the instructions, but before I could transmit them, the bots began unpacking the crates. "What are they doing?"

"We're following your instructions, sir." The android nearest me said in a calm woman's voice.

"But I didn't send them to you."

"Don't be too alarmed," Felix said, returning with my coffee. The first sip hit perfectly—nutty, with a hint of caramel cutting through the milk. "Any device that enters this house needs to be inspected for security concerns."

"Hacked, you mean?" I set the coffee down harder than intended. The casualness with which he admitted the intrusion threw me, and I couldn't help wondering what else he'd found.

"Rohan, I assure you I didn't access anything inappropriate."

"You still violated my privacy."

"There are people who would trade almost anything to steal my technology."

"And that makes it okay?"

"It makes it necessary, Rohan."

"Then should I assume you've already gone through everything I'm going to ask you?"

He pursed his lips, and then our conversation was interrupted as Susan appeared on the massive screen behind the couch.

Despite my mental preparation, Susan's appearance struck me speechless. She hardly looked a day over thirty, wearing an Imgen tank top and jeans, with her hair in a messy bun. She was sitting on the same couch I stood in front of, but mirrored in a digital rendering of the living room—like a video call, except she was identical to the Susan from the videos before she died. Her movements had no hint of artificiality. And when the virtual Susan spoke, she sounded exactly like the videos too.

"Ah! My dear," Felix said, seeming as surprised by her arrival as I was. "I didn't think you were joining until later."

"I wanted to say hello before the interview began." She turned to me. "I'm a big fan of your show."

It never occurred to me that she might still enjoy media from our world. "Wow. Thank you, Ms. Craft—"

"Susan."

"Thank you, Susan. I had no idea that you watched it—or watched anything, for that matter."

She chuckled. "Hopefully, someday there will be enough other people in here for some native entertainment. But for now, yes, when I'm tired of building or exploring or working on the transfer with my dear husband, I admit I still rather enjoy earthside entertainment." She waved her hand, and a screen appeared on the wall beside her, replacing one of the windows, showing my interview with the drone manufacturing company.

"Is that the term you've chosen for those of us still out here? Earthside?"

Her face settled into a soft smile. "When I was pregnant with our first daughter, our midwife used it to refer to where we were and where my daughter would soon be. She was on earth, of course, inside of me, but she was not yet *of* earth. Just as I, too, am still on earth, living in the servers in our basement, but I'm not of earth anymore.

"Where are you of, then?"

"I struggled with that question for a long time. There were some obvious choices: Heaven, Eden, paradise. And some less religious ones like Atlantis, Elysium, or Shambhala."

"I liked Shambhala," Felix interrupted. "It felt like a magic spell as much as a location."

"So what did you settle on?"

"Meru. The—"

"Center of the universe," I finished. "Where the earth and heavens meet."

"Not just the earth and heavens but where the physical and spiritual planes meet as well."

"Feels appropriate."

"I still like Shambhala," Felix said. "All the Westerners are going to get confused by the pronunciation. Meh-roo? May-roo? Mare-uh?"

"They won't, dear, when you succeed and the world sees what you've created. It will be on everyone's tongue, in everyone's ear."

"What *we've* created."

"Would it be possible to get a tour of Meru?" I asked. "You've been vague with the details you release to the public. I'd love to see the world you've created."

Felix stared up at Susan with love and admiration as she answered. "Yes, I'd love to give you the grand tour. It's as important to show people the world that awaits them here as it is to show them that the transfer works." She waved her hand, and the entire wall of the house disappeared behind her, showing a slowly panning bird's-eye view of a majestic yet impossible city. "I've been quite busy."

"Is that where you want to start?" Felix asked me.

"I was hoping to begin a bit earlier, if you're open to it."

"How early?"

"With Susan's death and everything leading up to it."

Susan let out a quiet sigh as a dark cloud settled over Felix's face.

"I'm not sure that's necessary."

I knew he'd resist reliving this painful part of his history, but it was essential. "People only know what Irfan and Vance told them. You have to understand, most people still think you lost your mind." I leaned forward, watching his reaction carefully. "And possibly killed your wife."

"Absurd." Felix's nose twitched with anger. "Disgusting rumors. A horrible smear campaign to try to discredit me so he—"

"Then prove them wrong," I interrupted, not backing down from his anger. "You've had years to set the record straight, but you've hidden away here instead. If these are just rumors, if Irfan really did orchestrate a smear campaign, then show me the truth." I held his gaze steadily. "Because right now, their version is the only one people know. And your silence has only made people more suspicious."

Felix's jaw clenched, but I pressed on. "I'm here because I believe there must be more to it. But believing isn't enough. You need to tell your side of the story—all of it."

"Bah. The story behind science isn't important. It *works*. That's what matters."

"The story is essential for science like this to grab hold in the minds of the world. Technology-inclined people in particular will claim to want just the facts, hard and fast. The index card of details or prescriptive advice they can implement. But that's never what they remember most, or what they end up being touched by. It's always the human stories around the technology that have the deepest impact."

Felix glanced up at Susan, and I saw the hint of a smirk on her face.

"I told you," she said.

"Yes, yes. You'd think after so many years I'd learn to listen to you."

"You'd think."

Felix sighed. "Very well. From the beginning then. I shall tell you the heart-wrenching story of my greatest loss and greatest failure. The immolation of a once-great man, the toppling of a titan, the—"

"You're stalling, honey."

"I suppose I am. Very well." He gestured to the couch, where the robots had assembled the recording setup perfectly to my instructions. I settled in on the far side, pulling the microphone up to my face and taking out my notebook, as he collapsed into the opposite arm. Another android emerged from the kitchen to hand him a glass of water.

"Cut me off if I start rambling, will you?"

CHAPTER 3

SUSAN AND I MET IN THE FALL OF 1988. WE WERE BOTH finishing our studies at Stanford: I was wrapping up my computer science PhD, and she was finishing her undergraduate electrical engineering program. She was the teaching assistant for one of my favorite courses on computer graphics.

What struck me about Susan, besides her beauty and charm, was her creativity. She designed these beautiful scenes just by writing C code and shared them with me. We even passed a few games back and forth. Nothing remarkable—copies of *Pong* or *Tetris*—but it sufficed as a form of flirting among nerds.

I mustered up the courage to ask her on a date. It was terribly inappropriate, what with her still working for me, but the taboo nature of course enhanced the excitement. We caught an opening weekend showing of *Rain Man* and then debated its qualities over a beer and a glass of wine at the O. The bartender thought her ID was fake, and I almost accused him of being racist, but Susan talked both of us down. We got free drinks out of it.

Coming home to my apartment one night—Vance and I were living together at the time—I told him I was in love. He teased me mercilessly. We were like brothers. We shared everything, did everything together. I was worried he might see her as a threat to our friendship. But then he finally met her out at a bar a few weeks later, and when we came home, before he retreated to his nightly marathon of coding and gaming, he grabbed my shoulder and stared into my eyes with a brotherly love I didn't know was in him as he said, "She's the one, Felix. Don't fuck it up."

I did my best. We got married in Maui in 1994, and Vance officiated our wedding, neither of us being particularly convinced by one religion or another. We wrote our own vows, and though I can't remember every line, I do remember our core commitment: that no matter what life threw at us, nothing was more important than our love for each other. Most vows seem to focus on committing to being with each other through the bad, but we committed to being together through the good too. Somehow we knew we were destined for greatness, and greatness tends to take a toll on love. You get so wrapped up in changing the world outside your home that you neglect the world inside it. I needed her to know that wouldn't be me. If I had to throw it all away to stay with her, if I had to move into a shack in the mountains, I would do it. Love must always come before work.

The first few years were wonderful. We stayed in our small apartment on the bay, sharing stories from work over takeout, going to the movies, arguing about philosophy and science and technology over beers with Vance and others from school and work. The kind of simple, joyful life you can only appreciate after it's passed.

Sometime in our third year, we came home from the bar, and she turned to me and said, "I think we should start a family."

I was shocked. The thought had barely crossed my mind. And whenever it did, I told myself we'd get to it later. We weren't ready yet. But Susan rightly pointed out that these big changes in life either happen intentionally, before you're ready, or you eventually realize you're out of time and scramble toward them. Given the choice between an intentional, proactive life change and a reactive one, proactive was certainly better.

Our beer budget turned into a nursery budget. The takeout was slowly replaced by cooking at home, both to save money and to invest more in our health. I'd been promoted a few times at work and was leading the team launching one of the first handheld computers, an early predecessor to the smartphone. My plan was to see the launch through, then leave to start my own company. Our savings had grown, and I'd always dreamed of building something of my own. I knew it would only be harder once a baby was in the mix.

The launch event was a success, but no one bought the product. At the time, we had no way to access the internet on the go, and you couldn't do much on it anyway besides send emails. People were still happy to keep physical rolodexes, take physical notes. No one texted back then. We were, of course, right that a handheld computer would be a world-changing device, but sometimes being too early is no different than being wrong.

The company needed someone to take the fall, and I was the natural choice. I came in to work a few weeks later to two security guards and an HR manager waiting for me. I wandered the streets of the Mission, my box of personal effects swinging in front of me for what must have been hours, before I made my way home.

I debated the best way to tell Susan what had happened all day, but when I opened the door to our little apartment, the scene before me took my breath away.

She was dressed in a beautiful red gown, her hair done up, a touch more makeup than she usually wore. You have to understand, we spent most of our time in jeans and T-shirts, and she looked like she was going to the Oscars. God, she was—and still is—so beautiful. But I was completely lost as to what was happening. The table was set for dinner, a candle burning in the center.

I stumbled into the apartment, and she saw the box. I was so afraid of how she was going to react, but you know what she did? She laughed! Just laughed and took it from my hands and gave me a kiss on the cheek, then placed it in the other room.

"I'm sorry" was all I could muster.

She smiled as she uncorked a bottle of wine and poured me a glass. "Don't be sorry, sweetie. It's not your fault."

"I still feel like I failed you."

She kissed me on the cheek and handed me the wine. "You didn't."

"I'll find something else. Don't worry." I knew the market was shit and I'd have a black mark on my name in the industry, but I couldn't burden her with that thought.

She gave me the most tender, loving look and held my face with one hand, staring so deeply into my eyes. "No."

No! Can you imagine my shock? I was flabbergasted. I didn't even know what she was saying no to! But then she continued: "You and I both know you're destined for more than that."

"But it's not the right time—"

"It will never be the right time."

"We need to save more—"

"We have enough, Felix."

"I'm not ready—"

"You'll never be ready until you start. So start now. Do it for me." She kissed my hand and lowered it to her belly. "Do it for us."

I'm not ashamed to admit I melted into a puddle of tears. Joy for our child, love for Susan's faith in me, terror for what lay ahead—everything hit at once. It was one of those big cries where your whole chest and abdomen clench, gasping for breath, almost out of body from the intensity. But she held me there in our kitchen as our food got cold, and she started to cry, too, and then laugh, and then we were both laughing. And we collapsed on the floor and cried and laughed and held each other. It was one of the more beautiful moments of my life.

Impending fatherhood transforms a man. It brings new fears and insecurities, certainly. But it also brings a drive you didn't know you had. A focusing of your energy, as if your light were scattered by a prism before but now is magnified into one point: providing the best life possible for this child, and beyond that, creating the best world possible for them to grow up in. It's a terrifying pressure to be thrust upon you, but when a man embraces that energy and allows it to course through him, to direct his actions, there's nothing in this world he can't accomplish.

I thought I knew how to work hard before. I was wrong. The next seven months were the most productive, driven period of my life. I launched my first software product a week before our first daughter, Aria, was born. It took off like a rocket. I remember interviewing candidates over the phone, bouncing Aria in one arm, running on three hours of sleep, yet somehow untired from the adrenaline of it all.

Then we had our second daughter, Mira. Susan rose through the ranks of work. My business continued to grow. Then 2001 hit. We lost nearly everything—clients, jobs, savings. I drained the company accounts, trying to keep my employees paid until there was nothing left.

We'd always joked about it, but we ended up having to move to that imaginary cabin in the woods. It wasn't *quite* in the woods. I still needed internet access. But it was damn close. We sold the home, the cars. The business declared bankruptcy, and Susan took on the weight of parenting while I tried to dig us out of the hole.

During that period, I sat at my desk in the tiny office, leaning back in my chair to look out into the living room where Susan was playing with the girls. The funny thing about kids is that their imagination seems to increase the less you give them to work with. Fill a room with toys, and they'll hop from one to the next, never engaging with any of them. But limit them to one or two, and they'll invent endless games to play with them.

They had a couple of dolls—Barbies, I suppose—and every day they imagined new worlds for their Barbies to live in. One day, they were doctors. Another, they were mommies. They went on vacations to the kinds of places I had been so confident I'd be able to take them a year ago. I didn't know I had it in me, but when I stepped away from the computer to play with them, I was instantly sucked into their imaginary worlds. I developed a hunch that we adults still had that creativity and play inside of us, buried deep between layers of faux seriousness and decorum, but eager to let out if given the right environment to do it.

There were already games on the market where you could simulate people going through life: getting jobs, building houses, marrying, and so on. But none that you could play with other people. I somehow resummoned that intensity I'd tapped into six years earlier, and *Parallel* was born a year later. The difference this time, of course, was that I didn't do it alone. It wouldn't have been possible without Susan's experience and contribution. I built the back end for some feature and then took the girls while she hopped on and made it look beautiful and run efficiently.

Parallel took off even faster than my first business had. I was right that people longed for another world, one where they weren't burdened by the challenges of maintaining their lives, and where they could embark on adventures or creative pursuits they might not be able to afford in real life. The train was charging out of the station again, but this time I had my best friend in the locomotive with me. We spun up the new company, Imgen, a misspelling of the word "imagine" based on the available URL. Moved back to the Bay Area. Vance came on as the third cofounder. Soon, millions of people, and eventually billions, were playing our games.

Everything we'd dreamed of was coming true. And then...

We were in Austin for Aria's thirtieth birthday when it happened. She and her friends invited us out dancing late into the night, and around one in the morning, Susan fell.

At first, we thought nothing of it. The type of funny incident that happens with enough intoxicants and fatigue. But when I grabbed her hand to help her up, I noticed something was wrong with her grip. Her hand couldn't quite close around mine.

She sensed it, too, and in that moment, the rest of the world disappeared. The music was gone. The people were gone. Even our daughter was gone. Our eyes were locked in silent terror.

Aria's husband helped me scoop her up and carry her out of the club, and we went straight to the hospital. They tried to tell us she was drunk and had fallen, that it was nothing, but I insisted. I'm not proud of how I treated the staff that night. I was scared, terrified, and I took my fear out on them. They were on the verge of throwing us out when Vance arrived. He was a major donor to the hospital through the university, and he pulled some strings to get us checked in and given the best care possible.

I didn't sleep that night. I couldn't. I was paralyzed by the need to act, but the inability to do so. I was half drunk from exhaustion and fear when the doctor returned in the morning. He handed us a tablet and let us swipe through the scans as he delivered the news in a practiced yet alienating calm. Brain cancer.

You don't realize how much you take your partner's future for granted until it's ripped away from you. You have all these little fantasies about growing old together, bouncing your grandchildren on your knees, sitting on a porch holding each other's hands while watching the sunset. You know death will come for you both someday, but it's far enough away to forget about it.

Then reality comes crashing down, and you discover the fantasies truly were just that: fantasies. You think about where you were a year ago and realize how shockingly short a time it's been. All these days, weeks, months that slipped like sand through your fingers, when you could have been holding them, appreciating them, loving them, but you wasted them, thinking you had more time than you did.

She was so strong. She wanted to make the most of her last year, to spend it with me and the children. To see her first grandchild born. And I...I didn't let her. I couldn't accept it. I knew I could never live with myself if I didn't try everything in my power to stop it from happening. Genius, greatness, whatever you want to call the gift that I have, it can be a curse sometimes. When you believe you have the power to shape the world according to your will, you cannot accept things others might.

For weeks, I barely slept, consumed by research. Traditional treatments, experimental drugs, alternative therapies. I explored everything. But nothing offered hope. Then one night, staring at Susan's brain scans, a wild thought struck me. What if the problem wasn't saving her body but saving her mind? All those years of studying consciousness, those philosophical debates with Vance about the nature of identity—what if they'd been preparing me for this moment?

And so began the hardest challenge of my life. Ending death. Trying to spare myself, my children, and the world from the grief I could not bear to endure.

Felix let out a long breath and stroked the side of his arm, a self-soothing gesture I'd seen him do subconsciously a few times throughout our conversation. "Do you mind if we break for a moment?"

"Certainly." I was impressed he had made it through the entire story without much of a pause. Even though the events happened years or decades ago, the emotional toll of each one was immense. Taken together, I felt like I was starting to get a better picture of who Felix was, what drove him, and how he'd ended up where he was.

"Let's grab more coffee, shall we?" He waved off one of the bots as he said it, then walked to the kitchen. I hung back a moment to give him some space. I could sense he needed room to breathe, to recenter himself.

As he left, Susan appeared on the screen in the living room momentarily. I hadn't realized she was listening, but it shouldn't have been surprising. She didn't say anything, just gave me a quiet nod of gratitude and mouthed *thank you*, then disappeared again. It seemed odd that she would keep her presence secret from Felix. But perhaps it was easier for him to discuss this trying period without her there.

He returned a few minutes later with two cortados. After a minute, I said, "You've never shared this side of you before."

"The sappy romantic side?" A slight grin twitched at his mouth as he said it.

"The human side."

He nodded slowly. "No one's pushed me to share it before. It was always about the business. Technology is like a religion to so many people today. They saw me as one of its prophets and wanted me to stay on script."

"Or maybe they were afraid to challenge you."

Felix chuckled. "Maybe so."

I wanted to continue the story, but something had been nagging at me since he called. "I've been meaning to ask, why now? Are you dying?"

"No, not dying, but there's urgency. Have you seen what Vance has been reporting from those California farms?"

It had come up in my research the last couple of days as I tried to learn more about the end of their friendship. "His plague theories? Come on."

"You know the saying: 'One of the scariest things you can hear is that Vance was right.' He's cried wolf before, but he also has a unique talent for identifying trends early. And this time, the data troubles me."

"I'm not sure his wins mean much. If you keep predicting a catastrophe is going to happen, you're bound to be right eventually."

"That's true, but I don't think he's wrong this time. I've seen the reports from that one hospital, the man who was among the first infected."

"And what? You need to solve transference now so you can save the world?"

He chuckled again. "Something like that."

I leaned forward. "Last I heard, it was only a few patients. They suffered a grotesque fate, yes, but it hardly seems like a civilization-ending plague."

"Many more are infected than are being reported."

"So Vance claims."

"I trust him."

"Do you? Or are you using this pandemic theory to create urgency around your transfer technology? Because that would be—"

"Opportunistic?" Felix's eyes flashed. "Or prudent? I admit the existential risk is low. Single-digit percentages. But if it's as bad as Vance thinks, it could be a civilization-ending event. Worse than the Black Death."

"How could it be worse than the Black Death? We have antibiotics, robots, modern medicine."

"All true. However, society is much more interconnected now than it was during the black death. If one farmer died in 1800, the only people who starved were his family, and maybe not even them. But for every one farmer today, one thousand people rely on them for food. Now extrapolate that concentration to every other industry, and consider in particular what it means for people living in cities. The geographic area of a city cannot sustain its population. There isn't enough water and food there. If those supply chains are sufficiently disrupted, cities can break down in a matter of weeks. We saw a baby version of this in 2020, but compared to the potential of what could happen, that was a fairly small pandemic."

"What has you concerned about this one, then?"

"If it is a highly infectious, antibiotic-resistant bacteria transferred via food, then quite simply, we're fucked. The farmers will die first—they're often rather unhealthy anyway—and then their crops will die, cities will devolve into chaos, and civilization as we know it will be reset. Not completely. Some people will survive, but not enough to keep our current society going. They won't be running lithium mines or launching satellites. But as I said, I'm less than 10 percent confident anything truly bad is going to happen. If it does, though, we will need a way to save those who cannot be spared from the plague. It will be the only way to maintain some semblance of civilization."

"And you believe transferring is that salvation."

"I'm no messiah. But wouldn't you rather have a guaranteed afterlife than a theoretical one? If you were dying, being devoured from the inside out?"

I chewed on the question for a moment. My own mortality was still something I preferred to push to the back of my mind, easier to ignore than grapple with. "I suppose I'd like to have the option."

"Yes, yes." Felix's eyes glinted. "Everyone underestimates how desperate they'll be for a way out on their deathbed."

"Are you worried about the pushback from religious and spiritual communities? Some of them have argued that you're desecrating people's souls or bodies by attempting this. That the idea of a soul in a machine is absurd."

Felix nodded. "And what do you think?"

I looked around the room, my eyes lingering on a golden lotus on the coffee table. "I don't think it's that simple. You haven't talked about it publicly, but from observing what you've chosen to feature in your house, I can tell you're a spiritual man in a sense. You've alluded in previous interviews to an experience that shattered your view of reality, that convinced you of some kind of immortal soul."

"I worry that might alienate more of your audience than convince them."

"On the contrary. I think we're all secretly yearning for some way to marry our fascination with technology and our connection to, or lack of, a spiritual sense of the world. If you have a perspective people haven't heard before, you should share it."

Susan reappeared behind Felix, and he seemed to sense her presence. He turned back to look at her, and she nodded her encouragement again.

"Very well. A brief detour to the time I met with Death."

CHAPTER 4

I NEVER CONSIDERED THE NATURE OF CONSCIOUSNESS until college. As a teenager, I carried the overconfident atheism that plagues so many well-educated people. They fall into the trap of believing that simply because they cannot explain something using the limited scientific and rational tools at their disposal, that thing must be nonsense. I sneered down my nose at those who believed in something greater. How foolish I was!

You know that's where the term *sophomore* comes from? Someone *sophomoric* is pretentious and juvenile, at the top of the Dunning-Kruger curve. They've glimpsed the surface of knowledge and believe they know its depths. And to be honest, I would have continued in my sophomoric certainty that I understood the world and could deduce its mysteries through the rigorous application of science, but thankfully God had other plans for me.

It was during my sophomore year, by chance, that it happened. Vance and I ventured north to the redwood forest and took a "heroic dose" of mushrooms. Three or four grams, mixed in a tonic with lemon juice. As the medicine took hold, we began wandering, holding our palms to the behemoth trees, drinking in their beauty, until we settled down in the brush and ferns, our eyes growing heavy from the pull of the internal voyage.

As the intensity of the experience peaked, I was thrust into a realm I'd never seen before. At first I thought I'd opened my eyes because it looked quite like the forest I'd been in. But I was standing. My clothes had changed, and though Vance was gone, I was not alone.

Directly ahead of me was a woman—young and beautiful, with golden hair and pale skin. She was naked except for a midnight-black hood and a cloak draped around her. Her skin was almost translucent, the edges of her skull, her collarbones, and the outline of her pelvis faintly visible as the light caught her. I knew who she was in an instant. Death stood before me, but I wasn't afraid. I could tell she wasn't there for me—rather, she had something important to show me.

She beckoned for me to follow before she led me down a wooded path. We walked in silence, the only sounds my breath and the crunch of leaves beneath my feet, until we reached a small cabin, tucked away in the shade.

Before we entered, Death turned to me and whispered, "Don't be scared." Her voice was faint, calm, delicate. I nodded and followed her inside, and there we found another young woman, lying in a grand bed, a handsewn quilt pulled up to her neck. The scent of lavender and earth filled the cabin, plants and flowers crawling around the interior walls.

Death approached her and kissed her forehead, then beckoned for me to join them. I was confused but approached the opposite side of the bed nonetheless, and when the woman turned to meet my gaze, I nearly fell over.

The gray in her hair was gone, the bags under her eyes and on her wrinkled forehead smooth, her teeth perfect, yet the face was unmistakable. It was my grandmother, on my mother's side, restored to her younger self.

"No..." I whispered as I realized what it meant and staggered backward.

But she smiled at me with the full warmth of love you only find in a parent or grandparent, and she reached out from beneath the quilt, grabbing my hand before I could escape her. Her grip was shockingly firm. And she whispered back, "It's okay."

Death stroked her hair and spoke again. "She's ready. You don't need to be afraid, Felix."

"You can't go" was all I could think to say. I didn't believe what I was seeing. I'd been with her only a few weeks ago. She'd been perfectly healthy.

"Sometimes you can't plan for these things," Grandma replied. "But they happen all the same."

"You won't make it in time to say goodbye," Death said, staring at my grandmother with love. "So she asked if I could bring you here."

"I wanted to tell you how proud I am of you, Felix," Grandma said, kissing my hand again. "And I need you to be strong for me, for Paul, and for Ginny. They're going to need you to help them get through this. I won't have time to say goodbye."

A cry broke through the moment from the corner of the room. I spun to look for the source and saw a carved wooden bassinet, slowly rocking by the door where I'd entered.

Death walked to it and reached in to stroke the baby's hair. "He's excited to see you."

"I'm excited to meet him too," Grandma whispered. She tried to lift her head out of the bed to see into the bassinet but fell back on the pillow.

She rubbed her thumb along the ridges of my hand and said, "Tell Paul that Caleb and I are waiting for him, but there's no rush. We can wait a long time." Then she chuckled. "Forever if we have to."

"Who's...who's Caleb?" I stuttered, but her hand slipped through my grasp, as if her body had become air.

The walls of the cabin flickered, and Death said, "It's time to go."

"Who's Caleb?" I repeated frantically.

But Grandma ignored the question. "I love you, Felix. I love you so much. Be strong for them."

As hard as I tried to will her to stay, she kept fading, and soon she, Death, and the cabin all disappeared. My eyes flew open, for real this time, and though my vision still felt fuzzy, the trees swaying gently, I saw a pair of eyes staring down at me.

It was Vance. He said I was screaming, "Wait!" but he was worried about waking me. He helped me sit up, and I ran my fingers through the grass, trying to process what had happened, still unsure which world I was in.

You might think I took it seriously and rushed home to make sure my grandmother was okay. But no. As the vision faded, it started to feel silly. I was still a devout member of the Church of Science, convinced our brains and minds were well understood by biology and physics and that some sort of spooky communication at a distance was impossible. Obviously, I had not met Death. My grandmother could not have spoken to me. I was on drugs!

I told Vance what had happened, and he urged me to act. He wasn't quite the skeptic I was. But I brushed him off. God, how I wish I'd listened to him.

We took our time walking back through the forest to our car and stopped for a burger on the way home. When I got to my dorm, one of the RAs grabbed me. He said my father had just called. It sounded urgent.

My stomach dropped. My hands went cold. My rational mind refused to believe anything could have happened. It didn't make *sense.* But some deeper, intuitive part of me knew better.

I rushed to the common room and pulled one of my

dormmates off the shared phone. I dialed my parents' house as fast as I could, but neither of them picked up. Instead, it was my old neighbor. My father had asked him to wait by the phone in case I called. There was an accident. It was bad. He told me they were rushing to the hospital.

I flew back out of the dorm, grabbing Vance's car keys as I went. I was closer to the hospital, so I managed to make up for the lost time, and I nearly collided with my parents at the entrance. My mother was distraught, trying her best but failing to control her breathing as we rushed down the hallway searching for the room. A doctor met us at the door. We were too late.

My grandfather, Paul, arrived a few minutes later. He'd been on a job when they tried to call his work. He was a sturdy, stoic man, still pouring concrete despite his age. I'd never seen him cry before. Even his laughs were rarely more than a single *ha*. But he broke. Seeing such a man blubbering on the ground changed something in me. Made me realize there was a depth to love I hadn't yet learned.

I wrestled for days with what to do about the conversation with my grandmother. My rational brain still refused to believe it, but I knew I couldn't keep it from my grandfather. So at the wake, I waited until he had a moment alone and made my approach. Every detail remains clear—his blue shirt, the white lilies by her casket.

He was a religious man, so I massaged the story in a way to make it more palatable. I said she came to me in prayer and told me she was okay, that she was with God, and said how much she loved him.

He broke down again, after having held it together for most of the service. I wrapped him in a hug, his tears hot on my neck. I debated not asking, worried about what it might do to him. But I had to. I had to know.

"Grandfather...who's Caleb?"

It's hard to describe the spectrum of emotions that passed through his eyes in a matter of seconds. First shock, then sorrow, and finally confusion.

His voice was a gravelly whisper. "How...how do you know that name?"

My pulse raced. For a moment, I debated deflecting, but there was no turning back. "She told me that she and Caleb would be waiting for you when your time comes. And that... she was excited to see him."

Fresh tears began to pool in his eyes, and without speaking, he reached into his jacket pocket and retrieved a photo. It was black and white, badly worn by time, but the figures in it were unmistakable. It took all my strength to resist gasping.

In the photo was my grandmother, her face and hair the same as I'd seen in the cabin, holding a baby, under the same quilt.

"She really came to you," he whispered, delicately stroking the edge of the photo with his thumb. "Caleb was...our son. He would have been two years older than your mother. But he didn't survive the journey."

If I had any doubts before, now my view of reality was well and truly shattered. I pulled him into another hug as he looked at the picture over his shoulder, unsure if I was crying for the knowledge of my lost uncle or for how lost in the world I suddenly felt.

Over the following days and weeks, I ran through all the possibilities to try to explain away the experience. Maybe I saw the photo sometime in my youth and the image stuck with me, and it was some kind of freak coincidence that I had a vision of her death just before she died. But I asked my mother about the photo, and not only had she never seen it either, but they'd never told her about Caleb. Perhaps that sounds absurd, but that's the kind of hardened Great Depression-era people they were. My grandfather didn't doubt the story for a second, at least the version he heard. He was convinced I'd been touched by God, and until he died he kept pushing me to join the clergy. Believed I had a gift that needed to be cultivated, shared with the world.

Obviously, I went in a different direction. But the experience shook me to my core. No matter how I tried to twist my way out of it, there was no denying that something exceptional had happened. Something that defied all scientific explanations but hinted at a hidden truth known to sages and prophets and mystics, that I'd been so eager to dismiss. The world was stranger than I knew, and I desperately wanted to understand it.

It lay dormant for decades, but I always found myself pulled toward studying consciousness and the mind in my free time outside of work. Never quite sure what I would do with all the knowledge I was collecting, yet driven to collect it nonetheless.

But now I know. The universe has been guiding me, training me, preparing me for this moment.

※ ※ ※

Despite the emotional weight of the event, the memory seemed to make Felix happy, not sad. As though he saw it as a gift that he got to have that last moment with his grandmother, the kind of final goodbye so many people wish they'd had but never did.

"You can see, I suppose, why I haven't shared that story much," Felix said, breaking the silence.

"I don't think you're crazy, if that's what you're wondering. But I do think there are more likely explanations."

"I fried my brain with too many psychedelics?"

"No, not that." I kept my tone measured. "You had a powerful experience while under the influence of hallucinogens. The timing of your grandmother's death is remarkable. I'll grant you that. But you're asking me to believe this proves consciousness exists beyond the brain?"

Felix's eyes narrowed slightly. "Proves? No. But it hints at *something.*"

"Maybe. Maybe not. Our minds are excellent at finding patterns, especially when grief is involved. You saw a photo at some point in your childhood, even if you don't remember it, and your brain constructed a narrative during an altered state."

"But Caleb—"

"Could have been mentioned in passing when you were young. The subconscious picks up more than we realize." I leaned forward. "And we *do* have evidence of psychedelics unlocking long-lost memories. You're building an entire scientific theory on what amounts to an anecdote. A moving one, certainly, but hardly empirical evidence."

"Empiricism can blind us to other forms of knowledge," Felix countered, his voice taking on a defensive edge.

"Or protect us from building castles on sand. You're telling me the basis for transferring human consciousness into machines started with a mushroom trip?"

"Well, it wouldn't be the first major technological advancement that came about that way, would it? But it didn't end there. And there is more, of course."

I nodded for him to continue.

"It's a crude separation, but you might split theories of mind into two camps. One is the biologically constrained theories, where our mind or consciousness is a product of our biology. If our brain shuts off, our consciousness ends.

"Then there are the non-biologically constrained theories. These posit that our consciousness, mind, spirit, and soul are something super-biological that either inhabits our bodies or connects to the earth through them.

"Don't be deceived by thinking that the first category, biologically constrained, is the scientific theory, and the latter is the religious theory. Some Eastern meditative disciplines see our consciousness as an illusion that can be dispelled through intense practice. And some scientists believe there's an argument for consciousness as a form of energy or quantum-level phenomenon that transcends our limited understanding of biology.

"If our consciousness is biologically constrained, then it is not possible to ever transcend our bodies. We might create a perfect copy of our mind inside a machine, as I did with Susan, but we can never make that essential leap.

"But I do not believe our consciousness is biologically constrained, and I do believe the leap is possible. I started with the story about my encounter with Death because that was my first clue that there might be something more to how our minds interface with reality than we believe. I'm certain beyond any shadow of a doubt that my grandmother was communicating with me that day. But the question is…how?

"I started by exploring other reports on what you might call telepathy. Individuals communicating at a distance. And the overwhelming majority of them had something in common: shared DNA. I found occasional examples of telepathy between normal siblings, but much more often between twins. And when it happened between parents and children, it was much more common with the mothers than the fathers.

"The discrepancy in telepathic communication between mothers and fathers and their offspring seemed curious to me. One explanation could be that women are more emotionally in tune with their offspring and thus better able to receive their communication. But there's a better one.

"If you're worried about your child having some sort of genetic disease, doctors previously had to do an invasive test where they sampled the fetus's DNA through the womb. But in the last decades, they've switched to noninvasive prenatal testing, where they simply draw some of the mother's blood and centrifuge it, and they're able to draw the baby's DNA out of the mother's blood and test it that way.

"It turns out that even after birth, a mother keeps some remnants of her children's DNA in her body. Persistent fetal cells can be found in a mother's organs, including her brain, decades after her children are born, and children receive a small amount of their mother's cells too. They maintain a direct biological connection to each other in a way fathers and their children never have.

"If consciousness were somehow separate from our bodies, then our DNA would be the natural 'identifiers' for *which* body to tap into. A tiny residual amount of your DNA in your mother's brain might actually provide some sort of bridge between the two of you that allows this kind of communication or intuition at a distance.

"DNA is not simply an identifier, though. It's also a set of instructions. Your DNA contains all the necessary rules and guidelines for the construction of your entire body, including your brain.

"And what's particularly remarkable about those instructions is that they're constantly running. Every seven years or so, all the cells in your body are replaced. They die off and are remade, following those instructions that you carry within you. Despite this, when you think back to who you were a decade ago, you still feel like you. Almost every piece of you has died and been rebuilt, yet you're still you. You even have many memories that transcend that death and reconstruction.

"So what we think of as consciousness can continue through bits of the hardware being replaced. If it couldn't, then we would constantly feel lost, or we would have some sort of discomfort imagining our past selves. The type of alienation from our bodies people occasionally experience after severe head trauma.

"The classic thought experiment that captures this is the Ship of Theseus. If all the planks on a ship are replaced one by one, is it still the same ship? In the literal sense, not exactly because all the pieces have changed. Yet the *idea* of the ship persists. And if someone didn't know you had replaced all the parts and it still looked the same, they'd have no idea it had happened.

"But there's a key distinction between the Ship of Theseus and the continuity of consciousness. The ship is being perceived externally. The ship itself has no concept of its own identity. Yet you very much do have a concept of your own identity. It is not enough for me to look at you and say you seem the same. You could have been replaced by a very convincing demon for all I know.

"I believe we need to tweak the thought experiment slightly. Don't simply imagine the ship. Imagine you are sailing on the ship. You're at sea, and you need to keep replacing the boards as they wear out. That's what your DNA is doing. It contains the instructions for building the ship and maintaining it, so it is metaphorically running around your body, replacing the planks at all times. Your consciousness is riding on this construction, and the primary role of DNA is to design a vessel that can host consciousness.

"The history of evolution could perhaps even be seen as a grand progression toward building a complex enough host for consciousness. Not intelligent design in the religious sense, exactly, but something not far off from it.

"So the next question was, what if we started rebuilding the ship with something besides wood? If you replace one plank with, say, metal, it's still the same ship. It begins to look different and perhaps function differently the more of the pieces you replace in this way, but viewed from the perspective of you as a passenger on the ship, it is still doing its job. It is still getting you to your destination.

"If our bodies and brains are vessels for consciousness and constantly repair and alter themselves to provide that home for consciousness, then it stands to reason that we could replace some of those biological elements. We'd soon prove consciousness could interface with digital systems—Susan's mind perceiving and interacting with the virtual world we built. But here's where things get murky: Is there a critical point when the passenger decides this is no longer their ship? When we replace that final biological component, that last original plank, will consciousness still recognize this as its vessel, or will it abandon ship entirely?"

"Hold on," I interrupted. "Your cells are replaced with other biological cells following the same DNA blueprint. But you're talking about replacing neurons with silicon. Where's your evidence that consciousness would make that jump?"

"Susan came close," he said quietly.

"But she didn't make the jump. And even if it is theoretically possible, you could never know for certain that someone's consciousness transferred. All you could ever know is that something that acts like Susan or whoever else exists in your computer."

"Which is why I must make the journey myself."

"And how will I, or anyone else, ever know it's real if you do?"

"All knowledge has some element of faith if you dig deep enough. 'At the bottom of the glass, God is waiting for you.'"

"Heisenberg wasn't risking killing people."

"Neither am I, Rohan. As you know from the next part of the story, I've already made the mistake of testing this on others first."

I drummed my fingers on my leg. I wasn't satisfied, but this wasn't a debate we could resolve through arguing. Felix was right that if this technology worked, there would be no way to prove it from the outside. There would always be some dose of belief involved. "The girl? Are you comfortable sharing your side of what happened there?"

Felix nodded.

"Go ahead."

CHAPTER 5

OUR DOCTOR'S BEST GUESS WAS THAT SUSAN HAD A year, a frighteningly short amount of time to solve such a monumental problem. But thankfully I had worked out a decent bit of the philosophical argument, and some of the technical theories, for why and how someone might be able to transfer their mind into a machine long before Susan got sick. I had tried over the years to convince others at the company to work on it with me, but no one was particularly motivated. We knew it would be a challenging, expensive problem to tackle, and given the muted reaction to virtual reality and the funds wasted there, our board was not enthused about giving me more money to burn.

It's a funny thing, building a company to a point where it can say no to you. I suppose not unlike raising children. One day they're little and you can pick them up and put them in a room when they're bad. Then one day they're grown and don't call you for a year because you were bad. It's both a great success and a great tragedy. You want what you birth into the world to learn to stand without you. Yet there's always that part of you that longs for the early days when they were dependent on you. When you were needed. When you could feel a sense of purpose by protecting them, helping them navigate those early, awkward years in the world.

I knew one brain wouldn't be enough data quickly enough to train the AI model powering the brain scans, so I went to the university in Austin and started putting up fliers offering to completely pay off anyone's student debt if they let me experiment on them.

You can imagine the headlines. You may have seen them! "Mad scientist preys on poor college students" was the general theme. But within a *day*, students lined up outside my office, jostling for position.

We turned an entire floor in the Imgen building downtown into a scanning room. Vance used his connections at the hospital to poach a couple of surgeons. Students would get the early version of the neural mesh connected to their brains, and then they'd sit in an MRI machine while jacked in and just think about *stuff*.

In the beginning, the tasks were simple. Imagine an apple. Now imagine walking. Twitch your first finger. Second finger. Third finger. Here's a sip of coffee. Now beer. A picture of someone you love. Someone you hate.

Eventually, we had to get rather creative in how we scanned people. We knew we needed some locomotion tests, so we developed an extremely powerful functional near-infrared spectroscopy device within a helmet to measure brain activity through the scalp. So you had these college kids walking on a treadmill with a helmet on that was so heavy it needed bungee cords attached to the ceiling to support the weight. We needed scans of people having sex, too, and *that* was a whole logistical nightmare, what with the privacy concerns. And you know, despite what you may be imagining, it's never the most attractive ones who agree to the sex studies.

We still don't entirely understand how it works, but one day the model started spitting out answers to what people were looking at and doing without being told. We could hook a new person up to it, and they'd look at an apple, and it would say, "Apple." It needed a brief warmup period for most people, but unless they had some meaningful neurological disorder, it could interpret most of someone's observations rather quickly.

The same quickly happened for thoughts. Hook enough students up to the scanners and make them read Harry Potter, and it began picking up the words and ideas people were thinking too. It usually led to some hilarious back-and-forth once it locked in on someone's linguistic thought patterns.

"I don't think it's really working."

"Oh shit. I just thought that."

"Oh shit. I just thought *that*!"

"Banana, airplane—fuck. Wait, what if it reads something I don't want it to say? Don't think about Diana. Shit. It knows. Shit, shit, shit—"

We had to start giving students a safe word they could think of to shut off the readouts. A surprising number of people chose "pineapple" as their safe word. I don't know why that is.

I had my fears that it would be extremely complicated to develop the hardware and model to accurately read someone's thoughts from their brain patterns. But within a few months, we'd gotten so accurate with it that students started refusing to continue with the studies. They felt we were violating their privacy, looking too deeply into them. Everyone holds some deep, dark secret they're utterly convinced would destroy them if their peers or community knew it, often forgetting that everyone around them also secretly harbors a similar fear. We were coming off the whole *canceling* mania, where students were getting kicked out of school for making silly jokes in group chats, so I understood their concerns. Funny enough, what resolved the issue was adding a big red button they could smack as they ended the test, which would delete all their personally identifiable data.

From there we needed to tackle the next step: creating a full digital simulation of reality that was convincing to a connected brain. One that felt *alive* to the degree they could no longer tell if they were in the simulation or awake.

Susan's brilliance helped accelerate this process dramatically. She correctly intuited that the easiest way to orient someone to a digital world would be to make them feel at home. So we asked students to bring pictures of where they felt safest. Often it was the room they grew up in, but sometimes it was a frequent vacation spot or their current dorm room. With a few pictures of the location, our 3D rendering tool could create a convincing replica of it, then upscale it to real-world quality.

Two things helped make these simulated worlds more convincing. First, we realized we could actually use the student's brainpower as a sort of off-loaded visual processing tool. We'd create a simple rendering of the room, and then as they looked at it, they would project their memories onto it, which the software could now read, and they'd fill in any missing details or correct any mistakes.

It was beautiful to watch. They'd turn around the room, and the paint color would shift, or a bit of clutter would appear on the desk, or a favorite sweatshirt in the closet. Many of them began crying as memories of their childhood they'd long forgotten flooded back to them.

We slowly started expanding the scope of the rendering. Their whole home, their neighborhood, their school. And once again, we were shocked by how quickly the AI could render these worlds simply by reading the memories of people hooked up to the device and what they *expected* to see.

We created a digital version of the university with near-perfect accuracy for them to walk through, and even made it modifiable and multiplayer so they could talk to each other within it. There were some interesting challenges there, like when two inhabitants had conflicting memories of how something was supposed to look, but it managed to figure them out without breaking the immersion, except on rare occasions.

I knew there was a certain amount of risk to what I wanted to try next. But as I've said until I'm hoarse, every student going in was warned that this could happen, and they all agreed to it. It's not my fault they couldn't anticipate the effect it would have on them. Besides, most good science has only happened by traumatizing a couple of people along the way.

Anyway, we knew the simulation wasn't sufficiently detailed until we could convince someone that they were no longer in the simulation. If a mind attached to it could not believe it was real, a detached mind certainly never would. There's ample evidence for this: the *uncanny valley*, wherein if something looks very human but not quite right, it elicits a sort of disgust and rage. It's a common problem in video games when the graphics are too lifelike, and it has been a challenge with robotics too. We see a related problem with organ donations. You often have to suppress the host body's immune system to a severe extent so it doesn't attack the foreign organ. Our bodies and minds know when something *isn't quite right* and react violently to it.

Well, I should have anticipated the consequences a little better. We designed a perfect rendering of the testing room, as well as digital avatars for myself and the other workers assisting me. One of the students, a lovely young woman named Mia, finished her test, and we told her we were waking her up. But then, instead of waking her up, we loaded her into the simulation of the lab. Then we went through a simulated version of the same steps we went through with the people we actually woke up: removing the helmet that connected her to the simulation, giving her some water, quizzing her on how she felt throughout the sim.

With each step that the simulation went through, we on the outside felt a little more elated. It was like watching the first time a rocket landed back on the pad or the first time a car drove itself. We were high-fiving and cheering. She had truly no idea she was still plugged in.

We finished the tests, and my simulated self sat her back down and delivered the news.

"Mia, I need to tell you something important. You're still in the simulation."

Her face went through a series of microexpressions. Confusion, then disbelief, then something darker. She laughed at first, but when our simulated faces remained serious, that laugh turned hollow.

"No," she said. "No, I can feel everything. The chair. The air. I just had water." She touched her throat. "I can still feel it."

"That's because the simulation is reading your expectations of what those sensations should feel like and creating them in real time," simulated me explained. "It's actually quite remarkable how—"

She stood up so quickly that the chair fell backward. Started touching the walls, her clothes, her face. Her breathing became erratic. Susan moved to shut it down, but I grabbed her arm.

"We need to see this through," I whispered. "We need to know what happens."

Mia ran to the door and yanked it open, then sprinted down the hall. Our simulated selves followed at a careful distance. She burst out of the building into the sunlight and spun in circles, looking at the perfectly rendered campus around her.

"Wake me up!" she screamed. "This isn't fucking funny. Wake me up!"

Students walking by turned to stare. Of course, they weren't real either, just NPCs the simulation had generated to populate the world. But to her, they were as real as anything else.

She collapsed onto the grass, hyperventilating. That was when I'd seen enough. I killed the simulation and brought her back to reality. Real reality this time.

The moment she opened her eyes, she vomited. Bile and stomach acid hit the floor as sobs wracked her body.

"Mia, Mia," I said, grabbing her, trying to help center her back in this world. She threw off my hands, ripped away the medical devices, and jumped off the table.

I ran after her into the hallway, but she was already sprinting toward the exit. A group of students waiting for their turn at being scanned had their phones out, recording her panic. Some were laughing, thinking it was just another student freaking out about the tests.

"Stop recording!" I shouted at them. "Please!"

But it was too late. Mia burst through the front doors of the Imgen building and onto Congress Avenue. Cars honked and their brakes screeched as she zigzagged through traffic in her medical gown. A crowd started gathering, with more phones coming out to capture the spectacle.

"Someone stop her!" I yelled, but no one moved. They just kept filming.

She made it to the opposite sidewalk and collapsed against the wall of the bank building, clutching her head and screaming. By the time I reached her, she was scratching at her arms, blood dripping from her fingers onto the pavement, trying to prove to herself this was real.

I knelt beside her. "Mia, you're out now. I promise."

She looked at me with wild eyes, her mouth flailing as if she'd become so uncoupled from reality that she could not even operate her tongue.

The crowd had grown larger. Phones were still recording. Someone was live streaming it. Whispered voices realized who I was.

Security finally showed up and helped create a perimeter around us. An ambulance was called. But I knew the damage was done—both to Mia's psyche and to our project's reputation. Before I even made it back to the building with her, my phone was exploding with notifications as I was tagged in the videos.

I'm a tad ashamed to admit that my first instinct was to run more tests to see if this was simply a one-time reaction or if other students would have the same response. Of course, no one was eager to let me do that, and all our test subjects quickly dropped out. Even Susan was hesitant to keep working on the project.

I check on Mia sometimes. She's never quite recovered. Despite my belief that progress without casualties is impossible, I've never been able to forgive myself for what happened to her.

I didn't know it at the time, but Irfan had been building rapport with the board of Imgen, hoping to replace me. With how intense the backlash was for what happened to that woman, this ended up being his perfect opportunity. The board politely suggested that it might be a good time for me to step away from all my duties and focus on enjoying my last days with my wife.

In another life, I would have fought tooth and nail against it, but I was drained. Susan's impending death was eating me from the inside out. I hadn't been sleeping as I raced to solve the transfer problem. There was no fight in me, so I accepted their suggestion.

The one request I had, which they thankfully agreed to, was to take whatever progress I'd made on the project with me—one set of the hardware, all the code, and the models we had built so that if Susan and I wanted to keep working on it, we could. They were very strict about my not sharing anything that we were doing publicly, but they said that if we wanted to keep working on it alone, they would allow it.

※ ※ ※

Another coughing fit seized me as Felix paused the story. "Do you have any water?" My chest felt like it was on fire.

"Certainly." Felix waved at one of the androids, which was already on the way over with a glass.

"Sorry for the cough. You're sure the medical scan was fine?"

He nodded. "I wouldn't have let you in if I were worried. You really ought to get more sleep, Rohan."

I shrugged. "I can sleep when I'm dead."

"Heavens no. You can sleep when you've *transferred!*"

I grinned. His confidence was infectious, and despite my lingering skepticism, part of me did want this to work. He had glossed over a troubling part of the story, though. "You just described watching a woman have a complete psychological breakdown. She was scratching her arms bloody, Felix. And your first instinct was to run more tests?"

"All life-changing advancements carry some risk. Imagine if we'd abandoned vaccinations because of the side effects from the first polio vaccine."

"So you can justify the collateral damage because if this succeeds, it will be a vaccination against death?"

"We've lived too long in the shadow of the dragon tyrant. Perhaps death is inevitable. But if it isn't, we won't find the solution if we're paralyzed by the fear of making a few mistakes along the way."

"Why isn't anyone else trying to do this, then? Why is it just you, alone in your basement?"

Felix sighed. "Oh, they are. I'm certain they're continuing it in secret. Irfan wouldn't let an opportunity like this disappear. And I know Tapper has his own skunkworks going.

"Darius Tapper? What does asteroid mining have to do with digital immortality?"

"The call to the stars is its own immortality quest. I imagine he wants to load himself onto a rocket and send it out to explore or something. He asked me one too many questions at a party once. But I suspect he and Irfan and whoever else haven't made any progress for the same reason I haven't."

"And what reason is that?"

He drummed his fingers on his leg. "Ethics, for lack of a better way to put it. I wanted to create a gentle transfer process, and I'm not sure that's possible."

His candidness surprised me. Despite his claimed remorse, he didn't seem to truly regret what had happened to that woman. Instead, he regretted what had happened to him because of it. "So you would have sacrificed more students?"

He huffed and looked out the window before answering. "This wasn't some gulag science experiment. We could have found people who were dying, too, instead of college kids. People who were much more eager to find an alternative to death."

"Why haven't you?"

"You mean after Susan died? When I was expelled from Imgen, I got a…stern talking-to from some authorities about the extent to which I was allowed to involve others."

"So that's the other reason you're doing this. There's no one else you can test this on. It's your last shot."

I could see he was struggling to resist gritting his teeth as he responded. "You might say that."

I waved my hand, worried I might have pushed him too far. "Was this when you and Vance had your falling out?"

"Indeed. Vance was caught up in the managerial shuffle along with me. He'd been helping on the project, of course, and Irfan saw an opportunity to kill two birds with one stone. Vance had already gotten…darker at that point—started to develop remorse over what he felt we had done at the company, getting everyone hooked on pieces of glass. And when he saw what happened to Mia, it was the final straw. I think that was when he decided what I was doing was some awful insult to nature."

"So he didn't help you when you continued the project here?"

Felix shook his head, and I could see the lingering sadness for his lost friend in his eyes.

"Do you think he'd ever change his mind?"

He sighed. "I don't know. I doubt it. Part of me…part of me hopes that if I solve this, we can reconcile. That he'll see this is a wonderful gift to humanity. That I'm saving people from a truly horrendous fate. They're the only people I truly care about, you know—Susan and Vance. Besides my children, of course. To lose both of them in such short order…" He seemed to consider something, then thought better of it. "I'm stalling, trying to avoid this last part of the story."

"I don't blame you."

"I appreciate that, but the only way out is through. Let's continue."

CHAPTER 6

WE TOOK A FEW MONTHS OFF, AND TO BE HONEST, I don't think Susan wanted to continue with the project. However, she agreed to go on because she knew how much I was struggling with the idea of losing her, and having something to throw myself into helped distract me from what was coming.

It wasn't significantly harder to turn the virtual brain-driven experience into a full copy of her brain living in the computer; all the parts were there, so we just needed to create a way for the data to persist once her brain was disconnected.

The first time we successfully did that, we encountered a new challenge: Susan's body had woken up, but there was still a copy of her living in the world that we had built. What would we do with her?

All three of us knew that the digital Susan was not really Susan. She was only a copy. There had to be some way in which she was limited, in which she was an imperfect rendering of the real Susan. So we began testing her, trying to figure out where those limits were and what the differences were.

We created our own version of Turing's imitation game. I asked the same question to both Susans separately to see if they responded any differently. If I asked questions about our past or about her personality or anything separate from the experiment, their responses matched perfectly. It truly seemed like they were the same person. The only time I noticed a difference was when I asked questions about physical experiences or things that had happened since we made the copy.

The longer these experiments went on, though, the more their responses started to diverge. Even though they had been the same person, the more time passed, the more they split into two subtly different people. I'm sure you've daydreamed about who you'd be if something different had happened at a pivotal moment in your life, yet you never get to interrogate that version of yourself. Susan got to meet one face to face.

What made it a tad uncomfortable was that I recognized a certain...dare I say eagerness from the digital Susan for the physical one to pass. She wasn't wishing for her death, but I believe each one's existence was quite unsettling for the other. And while the physical Susan, my Susan, could take some joy in the existence of her digital counterpart, knowing that at least a piece of her would stay with me after she was gone, the digital Susan had no such comfort. To her, the existence of physical Susan was a reminder that she was not entirely authentic, and a lingering threat that she might be wiped out so we could try again.

You might be familiar with Searle's Chinese Room thought experiment, and it became a constant question at the back of our minds through this period. Imagine you speak fluent Chinese, and you're trying to have a conversation with someone in another room. So you write out a question in Chinese on a piece of paper and slip it under the door, and a few minutes later, they slide back a response.

Everything seems perfectly normal. They respond with reasonable answers in fluent Chinese. But then you open the door, and you realize the person on the other side has a giant book of questions and how to respond to them, all in Chinese characters. They took whatever question you sent them, looked up the characters, drew out the answer, and sent the paper back.

So not only do they not know Chinese, but they had no idea at all what they were saying. They were merely following the programming that was given to them. When Searle proposed the thought experiment in 1980, the idea of an infinitely large book of responses was absurd, but we entered that world years ago. So was this digital Susan really thinking in the way my Susan was? Or was she merely an elaborate Chinese room?

It's not exactly academic, but I've always struggled with the Chinese room thought experiment. Searle wasn't claiming humans have some magical noncomputational property. He was arguing that following rules to manipulate symbols, no matter how sophisticated, doesn't create genuine understanding or consciousness. But watching Susan's digital copy, I started to wonder if that distinction even mattered.

If you've ever spent time with an elderly parent or grandparent suffering from Alzheimer's or dementia, one of the most unsettling things about the disease is how the person repeats themselves. If a similar topic or prompt recurs in a conversation, they might say the exact same thing they said a few minutes earlier, not realizing they already said it.

I think this hints at something about how the brain and memory work. We are constantly throwing out preprogrammed responses to our environment, but part of our memory's job is to make sure we don't repeat ourselves too often. What's so unnerving about this repetition from people with neurodegenerative diseases is that it reveals something about human cognition: it's not always consciously working out responses to things. Sometimes it's retrieving familiar patterns. We recognize this in physical tasks, like when you snap back to consciousness while driving and wonder who was in charge of the car that whole time. But it happens in conversation too. Maybe Searle's right that rule-following alone doesn't create understanding. But if our digital Susan follows the same rules as the original, produces the same responses, and even claims to feel the same emotions, then at what point does the philosophical distinction between the two cease to matter?

Anyway, philosophical tangents aside, one big question still lingered: whether we should try again. Wipe out the digital Susan we had created and see if we could run another experiment, another attempt to successfully transfer her over. We could have done the experiment without wiping her, of course, but then we might have ended up with two, or five, or a hundred Susans, all subtly diverging, all deeply uncomfortable over which was the real Susan, and all but one would have had to be wiped eventually. Unless, perhaps, there were some way to merge them, though we wouldn't have wanted to do that if we did eventually succeed, because then none of them would have been the authentic one.

I wanted to keep trying, of course, and worry about cleaning up the mess later. But the two of them teamed up against me. They asked me to be happy with where we'd gotten, not to push this any further, to let my Susan enjoy whatever time she had left, not hooked up to computers and machines. Digital Susan said she was going to leave and focus on Meru until physical Susan passed. They didn't want to keep feeling the uncomfortable tug between them, and digital Susan wanted me to give my full attention to my Susan while I could.

I did my best. Our long days working in the office, and then in our basement, were replaced by walking around the pond, watching movies, curling up on the couch together with our favorite books. The girls visited when they could, but they had families and work of their own they needed to balance. Neither of us knew how much to involve them in Susan's last days. Everyone regrets not spending more time with their parents after they're gone, yet despite knowing how widespread this regret is, people with living parents don't make the effort. And once your spouse is dying, you feel some obligation to protect your children from seeing their mother suffer. You don't want to rob them of their last days with her, but you also don't want them to have to carry what is very much your burden. You want them to remember her from when they were children, when she could keep up with them, when she could care for them, not the other way around. You don't want to shatter their illusion that their parents will always be waiting in the wings to swoop in and save them should something terrible happen.

Susan—or rather, both Susans were right. It was how we should have been spending that time all along. Those lazy days are some of my fondest memories. I was deeply grateful for every day we got to spend together, not consumed by the hurries of life that lull you into the illusion that your time together will never run out. Each night, our breathing would slowly sync up as we drifted off to sleep, and we'd whisper about how happy we were to get another evening together.

I think we lived together more in those three months than in the previous twenty years of our marriage. Once I took my eye off changing the future, I could appreciate what I had in the present. All the money in the world couldn't buy one more day back in that cabin at the old computer, taking turns programming and playing with the girls on the floor.

One day we were sitting out by the pond on our bench, watching the ducks swim by. The late afternoon sun warmed our faces, and the scent of water lilies drifted on the breeze. Susan lay her head on my shoulder. At first I thought it was simply a moment of closeness. But then I felt her go limp, the rest of her suddenly weighing on me as her head slid forward.

I spun to my side and grabbed her before she fell. Holding her shoulders, I lightly shook her, saying, "Susan? Susan!" But her eyes were closed, her mouth slightly agape, her breath faint.

"No, no. Please no," I whispered as I scooped her up in my arms and carried her back into the house. She'd been losing weight for weeks, but I was still shocked at how light she was.

I somehow stumbled down to the lab, with her in my arms, and placed her on the transfer bed.

"Susan!" I yelled into the microphone on the computer, trying to summon her digital self. And a moment later, she appeared.

"I told you, we're not supposed to reconnect until—" She cut herself off when she saw her body lying on the table. "Felix, no."

"We have to try."

"No."

"We have to try!" I was screaming, crying, I'd had so long to prepare, far longer than most people are blessed with, but I still could not accept it. Could not allow her to go.

"She—I—didn't want this." She was trying to be firm, but I could hear the hesitation in her voice. I can only imagine what it was like to watch her body die.

"Please, please help me," I begged her. "Please. She can't go. She can't leave me here. She's everything."

"It's time, Felix."

"No!" I flew to the computer and started initiating the software we'd run to create her copy. I thought that maybe if she were on the verge of death, that would be the nudge her mind needed to finally leave its current host. Perhaps if it saw another place to continue its life, then it would make the jump.

But then, to my horror, the computer stopped responding and started glitching.

"What…what's happening?" The words barely came out.

"She didn't want this, and I don't want this," Susan repeated. "Stop trying to fight it. Stop trying to fix everything. Let her go in peace." Then she disappeared.

"No, no. I can't…" I was gasping for air. Everything was falling apart. I couldn't breathe, couldn't think. But she'd taken control. I was locked out. I couldn't even try to transfer her again.

I abandoned the computer and pulled her against me, my fingers in her hair, whispering through the tears. "I'm sorry," I said. "I'm sorry. I'm sorry. I'm sorry. I failed you. I failed us. I failed the girls. I couldn't do it. I couldn't save you. I love you so much, Susan. I'm not ready for you to go. I don't want to be here without you. I *can't* be here without you."

Then she let out the faintest of sighs, and she was gone. I crawled onto the bed next to her and curled around her, as she often did with me when we fell asleep. I held her until I had nothing left.

Some time later, the screen above us clicked on again, and Susan reappeared. "You didn't fail her, honey. She—I—knew this was always a dream. One last project to work on together, even if it was hopeless. All she wanted in the end was to be with you."

"Go away!" I screamed, and the violence of my reaction almost threw me from the bed. "You're not her! Go!"

I can hardly describe the look of shock, confusion, and sadness on her face. All she wanted was to help me feel better. To cradle me as I was cradling her. But I couldn't look at her. Couldn't bear to imagine what could have been if I'd tried a little harder, been a little smarter.

"You know where to find me," she whispered, holding back tears. "I may not be her, but I love you as strongly as she did, Felix." She disappeared once more, and it was months before we spoke again.

"What finally brought you back together?" I asked as Felix paused the story.

"Time, more than anything. My wounds needed to heal. I needed to mourn the Susan from this world before I could fully embrace the Susan I still had."

She appeared on the screen in the living room again as we spoke.

"And what did you do during that time?" I asked her.

She spread her arms toward the simulated living room behind her. "I built all this. Figured out how to create a world here, confident that Felix would pick up the project again eventually."

A rough cough escaped me. "What happened when he did?"

They glanced at each other, and something in their eyes told me it was a trying period in its own way.

"I won't bore you with all the details," Felix said. "But suffice it to say, I took the next step neither of us was willing to take when trying to transfer Susan."

"Deleting yourself?"

He nodded grimly, and a shadow passed over Susan's face. "It was harder than I could have imagined. Seeing myself begging not to be destroyed, yet knowing full well it must be done. And knowing he, *too*, knew it must be done, nonetheless he pleaded against it. Every time I sat in that chair and closed my eyes, I didn't know if I would wake up out here or in there. Every time might have been one of my last few moments with Susan." His voice cracked. "But I knew it had to be done. It was the only way to make progress."

"What was that like for you?" I asked Susan.

She took in a sharp breath. "Unbearable. I reviewed the

data afterward and helped with the setup, but I refused to be present for each test. From out there, it's easy to dehumanize us. But in here, it felt no different than watching a loved one die earthside."

It was horrible to imagine, and Susan's expression told me how awful it was for her to endure. But having some idea of what he went through the last few years deepened my respect for Felix's commitment to solving the transfer problem. I couldn't say I'd have been strong enough to kill a version of myself dozens or possibly hundreds of times.

Felix sighed. "Maybe you'd finally like that tour of Meru before we cap it off?"

"Please. I've been very excited to see it."

"That will give me a moment to make some of the final preparations," Felix said, standing and moving toward the stairs. "I'll have the bot bring you some more water and maybe something for that throat."

"Thank you," I said as he disappeared down the steps.

Susan watched him go, a loving but worried look in her eyes.

"You're not as confident it's going to work this time?"

"It's not that." She was still looking off toward him. "It's more that I'm worried about what it will do to him if it doesn't. Losing me, part of me, was hard. But the continued failure since has been hard in its own way too. Watching him destroy himself over and over again..." She shook her head. "We've had to suffer in ways no person ever has before."

"Were you really okay with it?" I asked, studying her carefully. "Watching him create and delete versions of himself, potentially conscious beings?"

"What would you have me do?" Her voice cracked slightly. "I'm trapped in here, Rohan. And...I know there's no stopping Felix when he sets his mind to something. He's not perfect. No one is. But I love him. He's everything to me. I don't want to be alone here. And if he does pull it off…" She trailed off.

"Then what? The ends justify the means?"

"Won't they?" she said quietly, but I heard the doubt in her voice.

"Depends on what the means are."

Her lips curved into a soft, sad smile. "I suppose so. Come. Let me show you what I've built here."

CHAPTER 7

SUSAN SPUN ON SCREEN AND REAPPEARED IN AN ELE-gant emerald dress, flowing as if underwater, her hair styled in an intricate updo. "I thought I should dress up for the occasion," she said, turning slowly so I could see how the fabric rippled.

The lab around her transformed, revealing what seemed to be an endless expanse of sky. Below, a city materialized. Crystalline spires stretched high, their surfaces rippling with flowing patterns. The buildings defied physics; some floated untethered, others twisted into Möbius strip shapes that shouldn't have been structurally possible.

"Felix thought the promise of immortality would be enough to draw people to Meru. But I knew we needed more. Some people are blessed with the creativity to imagine what they could do in a world like this, but most need to be shown the way. I knew that if this Meru project were ever to succeed, I would need to create an exciting world to draw people in. To help get them past the fear of transference. This is Zenith."

Susan's voice echoed as the view circled a cluster of towers that seemed to be growing and changing even as I watched. "It's one of the first cities I designed, and Meru's central hub. It may look geographically limited like any other city, but each building expands infinitely, fractally dividing into smaller units to accommodate however many minds want to live here."

I tried to contain my excitement as we drifted toward the buildings. "Everyone gets a penthouse."

"Exactly. The coffee shop you walk into can be crowded or empty."

The perspective dipped lower, sweeping through canyons of luminescent architecture. Platforms extended between buildings where digital beings gathered. Gardens sprouted from impossible angles, wrapping through the structures in spirals.

"The people you're seeing are simulated for now, but you can imagine how alive this city will feel."

We passed over a sports center where a pair of people were playing what looked like tennis, but the court was monstrous, and the players were blipping in and out of existence, teleporting laterally across the court to smash the ball toward each other at impossible speeds.

"Want to attend a lecture by Einstein? Step into a building, and you're there. Want to explore the ocean floor? Just dive off one of these platforms. Of course, not everyone wants to live in the city."

The view shifted again, and I found myself looking at a sun-drenched coastline. Perfect waves rolled in with natural variations, and surfers rode the breaks.

Before I could comment, the scene transformed into a quaint alpine village. Snow-capped peaks stretched into the distance, and fresh powder blanketed the slopes. The village itself looked like something from a fairy tale. Wooden chalets with smoke curling from their chimneys, warm light spilling from windows onto the snowy streets.

"Winter sports without the chill," she said as we panned over the view. "Unless you want to feel it."

Dense forest replaced the mountains. A small log cabin sat in a clearing, surrounded by towering pines. A stream bubbled nearby, and a cozy interior showed through the window, with a few children's toys littered on the rug.

"The beauty of Meru is that it can be whatever you need it to be." Susan's voice was softer now. "Whether that's an endless party in Zenith, the perfect wave, fresh powder, or just…peace and quiet."

I watched as a deer emerged from the forest. It paused by the stream and lowered its head to drink, each movement rendered with incredible precision.

"Forgive me if this is a silly question," I said. "But having everything the way you want it all the time…doesn't it get boring? It seems some of the joy in life comes from not knowing you'll get what you want. From the unpredictability."

"Yes, you're quite right," Susan said with a hint of a laugh, some memory I must have triggered. "I thought it would take longer, but it only took me a few days to get bored with having everything I wanted. The default settings here try to mirror the normal variance of life on Earth, though with some reasonable modifications like flying and teleporting. But if you want to break off into your own instance within Meru, you're welcome to tweak it however you want."

"Tell me more about these instances."

The scene shifted, and Susan vanished. For a moment, everything went dark before my vision exploded with neon light. We materialized in what looked like a massive arena, its walls lined with holographic advertisements. The stands were filled with thousands of spectators.

In the center of the arena, two figures clashed. One wielded what appeared to be lightning, arcs of blue energy extending from their cybernetic arms. The other moved like smoke, their body dissolving and reforming as they dodged attacks. They struck back with weapons that seemed to materialize from thin air.

"This is just one example of what we call an instance." Susan's voice came from everywhere and nowhere. "Think of it like a pocket universe with its own rules."

The lightning-wielder launched into the air, their jump carrying them impossibly high before they rained down a barrage of energy bolts. Their opponent countered by splitting into multiple copies, each one moving with perfect coordination.

"In an instance, you can define any parameters you want," Susan continued. "Gravity, time flow, even causality itself can be adjusted. The only limit is imagination. Meru would be a mess if anyone could change the rules at will, so these instances allow you to create opt-in areas for anything from duels to orgies."

My cheeks must have flushed because she laughed and added, "Let's be honest. We know what many people are going to indulge in the minute they get here."

"Can you simulate other people?"

"Yes, but not real people. That felt like too much of a violation of others' privacy and autonomy. But you're free to simulate any person you can dream up. Or non-person."

Red light bathed the next room, a massive bed with black sheets in the center. Sitting on the edge facing the camera was a naked woman, or more accurately, a succubus, with petite horns protruding from her flowing black hair, framing her anime-like proportions. Her eyes flashed open to reveal deep red around huge pupils as she stood, and her pointed tail flicked around her body, caressing herself.

Her mouth revealed small fangs as she said, "I've been waiting for you, Rohan," beckoning toward the camera with one long finger, the nail sharpened almost to a claw.

My pulse tingled, and I almost forgot Susan was there before she laughed and changed the view again.

"H-how…" I stammered, trying to recompose myself.

"Your search history was part of our security scan."

"That's…not okay."

"Forgive me. Felix isn't the only one who enjoys a bit of theatrics. I hope you understand the promise, though. If anyone transfers into Meru, they won't need to create their own fantasy world. We can automatically generate it for them based on their digital footprint. The AIs powering this world can give them the perfect house, perfect activities, perfect lover, until they get bored with getting what they want. It would obviously be hellish to get your way all the time, trapped in a false heaven, but as a welcome package…"

"I get it," I said, trying to interrupt whatever other surprise Susan might be about to throw at me, painfully aware that this was all being recorded.

The scene shifted again to a mirror image of the living room I was in, with Susan seated across from me on the digital couch, back in her jeans and tank top from before.

"Are you worried at all that this might be *too* enticing? Many people will see Meru as a far better life than the one they have here. People might try to transfer prematurely, before they're dying."

"Wouldn't it be crueler to force people to live in a world of scarcity, starvation, car accidents, and the deaths of their children if they don't have to?"

"Babies have died from neglect while their parents were immersed in video games. You're using extreme examples to justify creating what amounts to a digital opium den."

"You're also using extreme examples."

"Perhaps. But aren't you worried about too many people checking out of life out here?"

"It sounds like you think your life out there is more important than my life in here."

I pursed my lips. It felt obvious that the lives of people in the real world were more important. If I were a consciousness living in Meru like Susan, I might not feel the same, but that didn't make it any less true. "Yes, honestly."

"What's so different, though? I have thoughts, wants. I can feel love. Is my life in here less important than your life out there? Wouldn't you feel guilty deleting me?"

"Yes, but less guilty than I would if I killed someone."

Susan shifted uncomfortably. "I understand. And I know many will feel the same way. But I suspect that sentiment will shift when people see Meru saving their loved ones from awful deaths."

"You're worried about the plague too."

"I'm surprised you're not more worried. You seem very smart. Felix obviously puts a significant amount of trust in you if he brought you here."

"Ouch."

"I didn't mean to be condescending."

"How's the tour going?" Felix must have emerged from the basement at some point during our conversation.

"Splendid," Susan replied. His return seemed to put her at ease.

"I think you're going to have trouble keeping people away more than convincing people to join," I said. "If it works."

"That would be a refreshing problem to have. It's been quite a long time since I created something people couldn't wait to get their hands on. I can't help but wonder sometimes, late at night, if I still have it. Whatever spark created this life we have and helped create the world we live in."

"I'm excited to find out."

"As am I, Rohan. Everything's ready if you want to move this party downstairs."

"One last topic I want to ask about before we do."

Felix looked cautious.

"What has your relationship with Vance been all this time? He was key in the founding of Imgen, and in your and Susan's relationship. But then he disappeared."

I could tell I touched a nerve. Throughout Imgen's rise, the photos were always of the three of them, with Felix and Vance seeming almost as affectionate toward each other as Felix and Susan. The deep kind of brotherly love you might only find once or twice in your life. And Felix lost Vance and Susan in such short order. It was no wonder he fell as hard as he did.

"We haven't spoken in years. He loved Imgen almost as much as I did, and I know it broke him to get tossed out. He didn't have the double whammy of watching his love die as I did, but he also didn't have anyone to share the hardship with. Vance has always been a solitary creature. I may have been his only close friend. And when we broke up, for lack of a better word, it did something to him."

"I have to imagine you weathered plenty of challenges over the years. Being expelled from Imgen must have been difficult, but why did that in particular drive a wedge between you?"

"Well, no relationship ends all at once. Cracks form over the years, and water seeps through them, widening them. The final break gets all the credit, but it needs a weakened target.

"When we started Imgen, we were both exuberant about the promise of a technology-driven life. Computing had changed both of our worlds for the better.

"But somewhere along the way, Vance stopped feeling like all this technology was a good thing. I think he saw how much time people were spending on their phones, how young men and women chose to talk to AIs instead of each other, how people looked for apps to solve their problems instead of looking to their communities. And he started to feel that maybe we were making the world worse, not better.

"I obviously disagreed. Every new era of technology has some rough patches while the kinks are worked out. When we transitioned from hunter-gatherers to farmers, we were ravaged by new diseases until we developed the requisite technologies for preservation and sanitation. When we transitioned from rural to urban living, we were again plagued by problems that needed to be solved. Horse travel caused awful manure buildups in the streets, which were solved by cars, which then introduced air pollution, which was solved by electric cars, which introduced the consequences of lithium mining.

"It's foolish to think any new technology will be a free lunch. Obviously, downsides will come with it. But just as we solved the old problems with technology, we can solve the new ones with more technology. The solution is never to go backward, never to abandon what we've accomplished.

"He humored my work on transference when it was about saving Susan, but I believe after she died and I continued to work on it, his opinion slowly turned. Something about ending death was a bridge too far for him, and he felt it was his duty to speak out against it. That's why you see him going off on this bacteria so much. He suspects, heavily influenced by his new bias against technology, that we've brought this plague upon ourselves. But once you look at the world through that sort of lens, you'll find confirmation everywhere.

"Vance helped build this world, though. He should be seeing it through with me and continuing the march of technology forward. It's going to happen with or without him, and it would happen faster with him."

Felix slid down in his chair and stared out the window as a cardinal landed on the patio, picking up seeds that had dropped from the bird feeder. I was deeply familiar with Vance's work and knew he was not the anti-technology luddite Felix was making him out to be. Rather, he believed in a different approach to technology, one that used it to enhance our lives in the real world instead of removing us from it. But like a scorned lover, Felix had built up this caricature of his old friend. It was easier to imagine he was an enemy or lost than that he might be right in his diverging values.

"You don't have to say it. I know I'm being unfair. The truth is, I miss him dearly. We did see each other one more time after we were fired. When I was in the pit of my despair after Susan's death, he showed up. Tried to talk some sense into me. I was drunk and angry and screamed at him, but when I sobered up, I realized he was right." He glanced lovingly at Susan. "I was so wrapped up in what I'd lost, I couldn't appreciate what I had. So many times I've debated picking up the phone and trying to smooth things over. But I can never bring myself to do it. He'd never endorse what I'm doing here. Not unless it succeeds."

"How can you know that if you haven't tried? You're a genius who solves impossible problems, yet you can't make a simple phone call?"

Felix chuckled. "Maybe I'm like a robot in that way. PhD-level mathematics turned out to be easier to program than walking, after all."

"Believe me. I've tried to push him too," Susan said. "But he's right. He's too stubborn, and Vance is just as bad."

"I would not have accomplished what I did in business if I were not incredibly hardheaded and unwaveringly convinced that I was right and knew better. Unfortunately, that same hard-headedness appears in other domains as well."

"Even with his wife," Susan teased.

"Oh, you're one to talk," Felix shot back, and it was the first hint of a smile I'd seen on his lips in quite a bit. Then he glanced at his watch. "I suppose it's time, isn't it?"

"Do you feel ready?"

"I do."

CHAPTER 8

FELIX LED ME DOWN THE STEPS TO HIS LAB, AGILE ON the stairs for a man his age. As we rounded the corner and his workspace came into view, I had to catch my breath.

The lab sprawled before us, a perfect fusion of cutting-edge technology and organic design. Curved workstations flowed naturally into one another, their surfaces gleaming with embedded displays. The walls themselves seemed alive, covered in moss that gave off a soft, natural glow.

"This is where it all happens," Felix said, gesturing to the space.

I ran my hand along one of the smooth desks. "It's beautiful."

"Form follows function. The organic layout helps us think differently about consciousness transfer. Can't map a human mind into rigid squares and straight lines, can we?"

In the center of the room stood what looked like a meditation pod, its translucent surface etched with intricate patterns that reminded me of neural networks. A small drone no bigger than a hummingbird floated silently through the air, recording the events.

"You told me about how the process works in general, but what is it about this test that makes you so confident it's going to work?"

Felix typed a few commands into the console near the pod, and it began humming to life. A progress bar appeared on one of the screens, counting up to one hundred.

"A leap forward like this…it doesn't happen gently. I mentioned that I was uncomfortable shutting Susan's brain off entirely to try to force the transfer. It always felt too risky. If something went wrong, I might lose her prematurely. But now I'm convinced that is a necessary step."

"How will that work?"

The progress bar reached 10 percent.

"Once the machine has connected to the mesh implanted on my brain, it will begin creating an up-to-date model of my brain and body. After the model is complete, I'll begin working through an orientation procedure, starting simple with flexing my fingers and toes and working up to forming sentences and running. The tongue is one of the hardest parts to model. It's often underappreciated for what an incredible feat of evolution it was."

The progress bar reached 20 percent.

"Once the simulation is confident that I've accurately recreated all the basic biological functions digitally, including the subconscious ones like breathing and pumping blood, then it will begin the shutoff."

"Why do you simulate subconscious functions?"

"Our mind needs to be grounded in some sense of biological self, even if it's fake, to feel comfortable. You won't feel like *you* without the thumping of your heart or the twitching of your leg muscles, even if you rarely pay conscious attention to those aspects of your existence."

The progress bar reached 40 percent.

"Then the shutoff will begin. By sending specially targeted electrical impulses, combined with administering a fast-acting but short-lived sedative, we can isolate parts of the brain and disable them temporarily. This part has to happen quickly. I can't risk being brain-dead for too long, or there might not be a second try. But the machine will work through the different regions of my brain, starting with the most basic and working its way to the center of consciousness, the frontal lobe."

The progress bar passed 70 percent. The entire pod was humming louder now, and bright light was radiating from it.

"Once the shutoff is complete, assuming my digital self still seems normal, then we'll sever the connection between the two. If my digital self continues uninterrupted, that will be the first sign that we've succeeded."

"What's the second sign?"

"What happens when we wake my brain back up?"

"What do you think will happen?"

"I'm not sure. It's an array of possibilities. But I'd rather keep those to myself and simply see what happens. Makes it a bit more exciting, don't you think?"

The progress bar reached 100 percent, and Felix took a sharp breath.

"I suppose it's time," he murmured, to himself more than to me.

"Do you need me to do anything?"

"No, no. Just be prepared for whatever might happen." He paused, then added, "Emotionally, that is. Who knows what will occur when the mind leaves the body."

As if on cue, the top of the pod rolled back, revealing a delicate cage where Felix's head would be held, a glistening helmet waiting above.

"I know we've only just met," Felix said. "But I want you to know again how much you being here means to me. Today was the best day in…well, a very long time."

The sudden closeness threw me off guard. As hard as I'd pushed him, he seemed to appreciate it. Maybe it reminded him of his arguments with Vance. "I'm glad I could be here for it."

Felix looked at me with a glint in his eye that somehow threw me back in time to looking up to my father. Then he clapped me on both shoulders and pulled me into an embrace. "Thank you, Rohan."

I awkwardly patted him on the back. His shoulders were bonier than I'd imagined. "Of course, Felix."

Then he turned to Susan, who had appeared to watch the procedure. "I'll see you soon, dear. This will all have been worth it."

She gave him a soft smile, the kind that said she hoped he was right, but she wasn't letting herself believe it yet. "I'll see you soon."

"Come, my friends! 'Tis not too late to seek a newer world!" Felix roared as he removed his jacket, folding it neatly on the table by the pod.

"To strive, to seek, to find, and not to yield," I replied, giving him a respectful nod as I stepped away.

He flashed me a proud grin and then lay down on the bed. And as the pod closed around him and the helmet descended on his head, he looked to Susan one last time before he was hidden from both our views.

The pod whirred to life, and a new status bar appeared on the screen beside it, indicating it was cutting the tiny incision in his skull that would allow the transfer cable to connect to the mesh on his brain.

"I hope I feel that one day," I said as the machine continued to work.

"The confidence? Excitement?" Susan asked.

"The love. He can wax about saving the world and slaying the dragon tyrant and restoring his name, but this story was about you. You're the reason he's doing this. His devotion to you…it's hard to comprehend. I always respected him for his mind. Now I respect him more for his heart."

"Well, that's awfully touching," Felix said from the pod.

I flushed with embarrassment. "I, ah…didn't realize you could still hear us."

"Only for a moment more. Ooh! Time to go!" The readout updated again and said it was initiating the simulation.

A digital rendering of the lab appeared on the screen by the bed, and after a few tense minutes, a copy of Felix's body appeared on the simulated pod.

The Felix in the simulation began moving his fingers and toes, just as he'd described. Each movement was precise, natural. If I didn't know better, I'd think I was watching a video recording rather than a simulation.

"Heart rate stable. Breathing normal," Susan reported, monitoring the various displays.

The digital Felix sat up in the simulated pod and rotated his head. Then he stood. He walked a few steps, jumped slightly, and ran his hands through his hair. Each motion was fluid, human.

"Now for the language tests," Susan said. Felix began reciting what seemed to be prepared phrases in multiple languages. His voice came through clearly on the lab's speakers, sounding identical to the man lying in the pod beside us.

"The brain mapping appears complete," Susan noted, her eyes fixed on the readings.

A new set of indicators appeared on the screens, showing a map of Felix's brain with different regions highlighted. The machine began its careful work of temporarily disabling each section.

The physical Felix lay still and peaceful in the pod. His breathing was steady, monitored by a dozen sensors.

The digital Felix continued moving and speaking normally in the simulation, apparently unaware of what was happening to his physical form. I held my breath, watching both versions of the man who had trusted me with documenting this moment.

The shutdown sequence began at the base of Felix's brain. The indicators showed each region going dark in sequence, like city lights winking out during a rolling blackout.

"Brain stem activity decreasing," Susan reported clinically, though her voice carried a slight tremor. "Autonomic functions transitioning to medical support."

The digital Felix continued his movements. He was examining his hands now, turning them over as if marveling at their detail.

"Cerebellum shutdown initiating," Susan said. "Motor control offline."

I glanced at Felix's physical body. His fingers twitched once, then went still. The medical systems took over maintaining his vital functions as more of his brain went dark.

"Temporal lobe shutting down…memory centers offline… occipital lobe next…"

Region by region, the brain activity indicators dropped to minimal levels. Yet in the simulation, the digital Felix remained animated and aware, now engaged in solving complex mathematical equations that appeared before him.

"Parietal lobe shutdown complete," Susan announced. "Moving to frontal lobe."

I held my breath as I watched the final region of Felix's brain power down. The readings showed nearly flat lines across all areas now, while the digital version continued to exist, apparently unaffected.

"Neural shutdown sequence complete," Susan said softly. "Brain showing minimal activity. Life support systems normal."

The lab fell silent except for the quiet hum of the equipment keeping Felix's body alive. His physical form lay still, but on the screens above, his digital self moved with purpose and awareness, as if nothing had changed.

"How long do we have?" But as I asked, a new countdown appeared by the bed, with fifty-two seconds remaining.

"Felix, how are you feeling?"

"I feel exactly the same, but we've heard that before. Go ahead and cut it."

Susan nodded, and the readout confirmed the link between his digital mind and physical body had been severed.

"*Nothing* feels different?" I asked, somewhat incredulous.

"The smells are a little dulled, but that's expected. We haven't figured out exactly how to simulate those."

"You get used to it," Susan said, her eyes locked on some data she was following from her end.

"What do we do now?" I asked, trying to tamp down the excitement that was bubbling up. Everything looked successful to me so far, yet they didn't seem to share my enthusiasm. They'd clearly been here before, felt this level of success before, and were waiting for the final confirmation.

"Now the final check," Felix said. "In every test in the past, I've woken up in that bed, normal as can be. If you're sensing a lack of enthusiasm on my part, it's because I know that most likely, I—the me in here—am about to be deleted. The awakening I've both yearned for and dreaded. Every past attempt, I—this me, anyway—have woken back up on that bed. But now I'm here..."

"And he's deleted himself countless times," Susan added. Suddenly their dour moods made sense. They were defense mechanisms, preparing themselves for the letdown that had awaited them so many times before.

"When will we know if it worked?"

Sedatives should start wearing off in a moment," Susan said. "Look." She nodded toward the monitors. Felix's physical brain activity was returning to normal. His breathing reached a steady fourteen per minute, and his heart rate returned to sixty.

The pod finished opening up and retreated out of the way, leaving Felix lying on the modified dentist's chair, looking like he'd simply fallen asleep. I glanced, unsure, at the digital Felix and Susan. Their eyes were locked on the body, waiting for any signs of consciousness.

"How long has it been?" Felix asked, and a stopwatch appeared by the bed, likely for my benefit more than his, showing 1:24.

"Longer than usual," Susan said.

"How much longer?"

"Felix has woken up within a minute every time before."

We watched the stopwatch tick up another thirty seconds.

"Rohan," Felix asked, "would you be so kind as to go give my body a little nudge?"

Nervousness, even fear, crept through me at the thought. Felix was right that we had no idea what might happen to his body if he had succeeded. I'd never seen someone die in person before, but would this even be considered a death? Not a spiritual one, certainly, and his body was still breathing. But I steeled myself for whatever may come and approached the bed, giving Felix's arm a light shake.

"Felix?" I said, a touch quieter than a yell. "Felix, are you in there?"

"Little brain wave spike," Susan said behind me. But his eyes didn't open. His body didn't stiffen or respond to my gestures.

My calm curiosity started to fade, and something primal in me took over. As far as my biological programming was concerned, I was looking at a dead man, or a dying man, who had moments ago become a friend. Intellectually, I knew that Felix's mind was, to some extent, still there in the room with me, but my instincts took over.

I began shaking him harder. "Felix! Felix, are you in there?"

Only minor blips in his brain waves responded.

My pulse raced faster. I tilted him up slightly on the bed and let him fall back, hoping the falling sensation would trigger something. But again, only minor brain wave responses.

"What's going on?" I asked, becoming frantic.

"It's not a coma," Susan murmured, still unnervingly calm.

"Why not?"

"We'd see no brain wave response."

"I'm certainly not *awake*, though. Rohan, get a little rougher with me, will you?"

"I'm not sure I'm comfortable with that."

"Oh, please. Smack me around a little. This is important."

I hesitated, staring at his body.

"Don't be a pansy. This is for science."

I cocked back my arm and unleashed a slap across his face, nearly knocking his head off the edge of the bed, before I grabbed his shoulders and recentered him.

"Remind me not to get on your bad side."

"You asked!"

"Only teasing. But look." The brain wave graph was still shockingly unresponsive. Even his heart rate barely moved.

"Cortisol is up," Susan said.

"What does that mean?" I asked.

"It seems as though my fight-or-flight response is still somewhat intact, even if my brain isn't fully responding."

"So..."

Felix and Susan looked at each other, and I wondered if they were having some silent communication without me. Then she gave the slightest nod, confirming my suspicions, and Felix said,

Rohan, there are some syringes in the drawer by the wall. One batch of them should be labeled 'spike.'"

"Spike?"

"It's a caffeine and theophylline compound. General brain stimulant. Might do the trick."

"If this goes wrong, it's on you, Felix."

"I think it's our last option."

"And if this doesn't do anything?"

"Well…then I suppose we'll have to think of something else."

"This is insane," I muttered, but I crossed the room anyway, finding the basket of syringes in the corner of a drawer. I pulled off the packaging as I returned to his bedside, looking to both of them for final confirmation before plunging the needle into his upper arm.

My eyes were glued to his face as I held the syringe against him, watching for any signs of reaction. The stopwatch quietly beeped the seconds behind me. I peeked at the heart rate monitor, and at first, nothing changed. But then his pulse started increasing: seventy, eighty, one hundred, one twenty.

"Felix?" I said again, more hesitant than demanding this time. His nostrils were flaring, tension running through his neck and down into his arms.

I took a step closer to his head and said his name again. Then, finally, his eyes opened, and he stared straight up at the ceiling.

"Drat," Felix said behind me, and Susan let out a frustrated sigh.

Something felt wrong, though. I looked into his eyes, and they seemed vacant, glossed over, like they were open but not truly seeing anything.

"Felix?" I asked again, leaning over his head to try to make eye contact. His pupils suddenly narrowed, and red seeped into his scleras as his eyes locked onto mine.

My body understood the danger before my mind did. Whatever looked out from those eyes wasn't Felix anymore. I tried to jump away, but I was too slow. He grabbed my wrist with one hand, his grip crushing, and yanked me back toward him.

His other hand shot up and wrapped around my throat, squeezing with inhuman strength. I gasped and tried to pull away, but I couldn't break free. No recognition flickered in his gaze. The man I'd been interviewing was gone.

"Felix, stop!" Susan shouted behind me.

I tore at his fingers. The room darkened at the periphery. Through the haze, his face contorted into a snarl, teeth bared like a rabid animal.

"Help...please..." I gasped.

Felix's grip tightened further, and darkness crept in. My knees buckled. A clanking sound echoed what sounded like miles away as what was left of my consciousness retreated to the recesses of my brain, fighting for the last drops of oxygen. Something heavy hit me, hard, and I flew off the table onto the floor and collapsed, gulping air between my knees.

I waited, terrified, for another assault, but it never came. And when my vision cleared, I saw one of the androids standing over Felix's body, one of his arms in each of its hands, wrestling to keep him on the table. As they struggled, another android sprinted across the room and grabbed Felix's legs, holding him in place.

"Sedatives!" Susan yelled, and I crawled as fast as I could across the floor, back to the medical cabinet. I pulled myself to my feet and searched frantically for something to knock Felix out, sending gauze and tissue flying as I looked.

Finally my fingers closed around a sedative, and I staggered back to the bed, ripping off the packaging and throwing it on the floor before thrusting the syringe into Felix's chest. He threw one last shockingly powerful buck against the androids, and then his breathing started to slow. His eyes lost focus and then closed as he went slack. I bent forward, forcing air into my lungs.

"I'm so sorry," the digital Felix said from the screen. "I had no idea. Are you all right?"

I nodded, still catching my breath. My throat felt crushed.

"What happened?" I wheezed.

Susan and Felix were silent, their eyes huge with shock. Then Susan slowly turned to Felix, and his eyes began to water.

"It worked," he whispered. "It really worked."

I rubbed my neck, looking warily at Felix's now-unconscious form. The monitors showed his vitals returning to normal under the sedation, but I kept my distance.

"I'm not in there anymore," Felix continued, and he sounded like he hardly believed what he was saying. "I'm…gone. I'm here."

"Then what the hell *was* that?" I choked out.

"A body without a soul," he whispered, consumed by awe. "Pure animal instinct. No thought. No mind. It's…beautiful."

"Beautiful?"

"Terrifying, yes. But beautiful too." His eyes were glossy as if he were in a trance.

"You set me up," I snarled between coughs. "You knew exactly what would happen and used me as your guinea pig."

"I didn't *know*," Felix spat, the spell broken. "But it was in the realm of possibilities. Surely you must have guessed at that potential yourself by now."

"Don't try to shift the blame. You deliberately withheld infor-mation." And then a darker thought crossed my mind. "You didn't tell me because you wanted this on tape. You wanted the theatrics."

"Good god, Rohan. I may be a fan of putting on a show, but

I'm not cruel about it. I thought *perhaps* my leftover body would be a bit…feral…but I didn't expect this to happen."

"Save it," I cut him off. "We both know you orchestrated this entire scene for maximum drama. And besides, there are other explanations. Your implant might have damaged your brain somehow. We need to scan your body."

"Yes, yes," Felix said, nodding. "That's a good idea. Roll me over to the scanner in the corner."

An android helped me move his body off the transfer bed and wheel it to the full-body scanner, which looked like a white donut with an Imgen logo on the side. It was a far more advanced device than the handheld one the android had used on me, and one that was standard in every hospital now. It could use MRI, CT, and a host of other technologies to do a rapid analysis of someone's body for any anomalies, from blood clots to cancers to infections. If something had happened to Felix's brain, this machine would catch it.

"How long will it take?" I asked as the contraption whirred to life.

"Just a few minutes," Felix said as I stepped back and started pacing around the room. I tried to come up with any other explanation for what had happened but drew a blank. Part of me, the scientist, couldn't accept what I was seeing. But there was another part of my mind that kept nudging me back toward belief.

Five minutes later, the machine began to wind down, and a message took over the screen next to it. *Felix Craft: Diagnostic Report.* Aside from the normal signs of age, it found nothing wrong with his body. His brain appeared perfectly healthy.

I told the AI assistant that he was in some sort of coma, and it responded saying that wasn't possible. There was nothing in his brain scan that would indicate anything was wrong with him.

"This can't be right," I said, reading through the report. "It says there's nothing wrong with your brain."

"And yet..." Felix mused.

"It should at least recognize you're in a coma. Wouldn't these devices pick up on that?"

"They would *if I were in a coma*. But I'm not. There's no training data for it to learn what a body without a mind looks like."

My heart rate quickened. The machine should have found something amiss, some clue to what had happened. But it was drawing a blank. It couldn't find anything wrong with him.

"Let's run it again."

"Wait, Rohan," Felix said as I closed the report on his scan. As soon as it disappeared, I saw there was another report below it. And while there was a green checkmark next to Felix's name, this one had a red exclamation point. The report was titled *Rohan Patel.*

"What the fuck—" But before I could finish the thought, I was consumed by another coughing fit. I steadied myself against the desk, chest tight with each breath. My throat felt raw, and I noticed a faint metallic taste I hadn't paid attention to before.

"That's a nasty cough you have."

CHAPTER 9

My fingers flew to click into the report with my name on it, hoping it said anything other than what my intuition immediately told me it was going to show.

Rohan Patel: Unknown Novel Bacteria: Positive. Est. 2 days since infection

Another coughing fit seized me, harder than before. A few drops of phlegm hit my arm, the faintest hint of blood mixed in. How was this possible? Was it already spreading across Los Angeles? Then the pieces started coming together. The robotics company worked on farming tools. The plant was infected. And the scan when I arrived...

I whirled around to face the screen, fury burning through the pain. "You knew! You've known since the moment I walked in here!"

Still coughing, I rushed over to the medical cabinet where I'd retrieved the stimulant and the sedative and rummaged through it, looking for antibiotics.

"You won't find anything in there to help," Felix said. He didn't sound like the same Felix from before. He was darker, more threatening.

"Shut up!" I snarled. "You orchestrated this whole thing. The timing, the stories, waiting until I was too sick to leave. How long have you been planning this trap?" I kept digging through the cabinet, and I finally found a bottle labeled *doxycycline.*

I ripped the cap off and started pouring pills into my hand. Felix's words from earlier in the day kept playing through my head. *Would you transfer if you were sick? Wouldn't you prefer a guaranteed afterlife to a theoretical one?*

"Don't!" Felix yelled from the screen ahead of me, and a medical report appeared beside him. "They'll make it worse."

"That's ridiculous," The word came out bitterly while I spun the bottle in my hand to find the dosage.

"Rohan, *look at the report,*" Felix commanded again. My breath caught in my throat as I felt another coughing fit coming on. I needed to stay calm so I didn't destroy whatever was left of my lungs. I took a deep breath and looked up at what Felix was trying to show me.

It was a preliminary report on what had happened to the first patients near the farm outside of LA. The medical doctor who had treated them seemed to think the antibiotics made their infections worse by destroying the healthy bacteria aiding their system, while doing nothing against the infection. The only patient who had survived so far had refused medication, aside from some immune boosters, and simply ridden it out.

"Okay, okay." My breath came in gasps. I had to do the same thing. I needed to get to a hospital, tell them what was happening, and demand the same treatment.

"Rohan..."

"What?" The word exploded from me, and another coughing fit struck. Fury boiled through me. He'd wasted the precious time I had to fight this.

"You won't win."

"I have to try."

"You *won't*. Look at the person who did. He was a nut. You haven't taken care of yourself ten percent as well as he has."

The man's markers flashed across the screen, contrasted against my own, which Felix must have stolen from my device when he hacked it. Where this man ranked in the top 1 percent, often 0.1 percent in terms of health, I was at the opposite end of the scale. In high school, I ran track and nearly received a scholarship for it. But I couldn't even remember the last time I'd run a mile.

"There's still a chance…" The words barely came out, and I only half believed them.

"There's a better option."

"This wasn't a pitch for the rest of the world, was it? This was all for me."

"Rohan, what I've created is an alternative for anyone on the verge of dying. A gift for the world. You are dying and can benefit from it, yes, but I also can't do this alone. As you alluded to when you arrived, people think I've gone mad. They likely won't believe I've truly succeeded at this. They need someone more skeptical, objective, to tell them the truth."

"You *have* gone mad!"

Susan appeared on the screen beside him. She didn't share the darkness, but there was still a stoic determination to her demeanor.

"And you!" I rounded on her. "You're okay with this?"

She took a deep breath and cast a fleeting glance toward Felix. "The world is dying, Rohan. So are you. I understand your anger. But think of how many people you can help. Think of what you can be a part of."

"Please," Felix continued. "Would you have come if I had told you?"

I coughed into my arm again. "Of course not."

"You would have gone to a hospital, and you know what would have happened there?" Felix and Susan disappeared, and in their place was a recording of doctors frantically running up and down the halls of a triage ward before a patient stumbled out of their room and vomited blood on the floor.

"You would have died like the rest of them," Felix continued. "The end of your life would have been meaningless. Another statistic. Now it can mean something."

"What do you want me to say? Thank you?

Felix slammed his fist on the digital table, and the echoing bang through the speakers was shockingly realistic. "I want you to grow a spine and help me!"

"Fuck you, Felix," I spat, wiping my nose.

The silence that followed my outburst stretched taut. When Felix spoke again, his voice had changed completely. The aggressive edge had dissolved, replaced by something that sounded almost like regret.

"You're right," he said quietly. "I'm sorry. I got…carried away." He glanced at Susan, who was watching him with a mixture of concern and disappointment. "This isn't how I wanted this to go. I won't force you to do anything."

Susan stepped forward. "He's trying to help." She gave him a sideways glance that hinted at a heated fight they must have had before my arrival. "Even if his methods are…"

"Disgusting? Cruel?"

She sighed. "He didn't infect you, Rohan, and what he said is true. If you hadn't come here, you'd have been dead in your apartment or a hospital bed within two or three days."

I looked at them. The shift in Felix's demeanor was jarring—from threatening to almost meek. Susan still had a disarming empathy I couldn't ignore. But something was wrong with Felix. Like his personality had shifted since he'd transferred.

"You're different now," I said, studying his digital face. "What happened to you in there, Felix?"

"I…" Felix paused, seeming to search for words. "I'm still learning to control my emotions in here. But think about why you came here today," he continued, his voice gentle now. "Your skepticism is well placed, but you know we're on the precipice of something incredible, and you have a chance to be part of it. You can become the first citizen of Meru, and as that first person, one who has a penchant for storytelling and spreading knowledge, you can be the voice of this new world. The one telling the story not just of the birth of paradise but of its cultivation. And what better place to do so than in paradise itself? You can be part of this. One of the most important figures in this new world we're creating."

"Stop selling!" My hands trembled as I tried to steady them. The worst part wasn't that Felix had so perfectly trapped me. It was that some part of me was excited by his words, at the grandiose vision he painted. At the thought of being more than an observer, more than the chronicler of other people's achievements.

The videos of Meru that Susan had shown me played through my mind. The sweeping expanse of Zenith, the impossible homes and mountains. All those hours I'd spent in video games in my youth, and admittedly adulthood, trying to escape my reality to live in another. Now that potential was in front of me, and not simply the unlimited freedom but a significance to my life I'd never considered but now couldn't ignore.

"Rohan, please. You might not have much time," Susan said softly. "This disease…it's horrible. And if it starts eating away at your brain."

I waved my hand, cutting her off. "Please just give me a minute."

Felix started to speak, but Susan placed a hand on his arm. "Felix, stop."

He looked at her, then back at me, and the fight seemed to drain out of him. "You're right. I'm being...I'm sorry. This isn't about me or Imgen. This is about you and your life."

"So that's the other reason you need me," I murmured, the pieces clicking together. "You need someone besides you to go through it before you reach out to Vance or Irfan. Someone else to vouch for what you've accomplished."

Felix nodded slowly. "Yes. But that doesn't mean I'm forcing you. If you choose to leave, to try the hospital..." He gestured to the androids by the door. "I won't stop you."

I looked at the open doorway, then back at Felix and Susan. The rage was still there, but underneath it, my mind was racing. I came here for a career-defining opportunity. And though this was a far cry from what I'd imagined, it was also much bigger. Not just reporting on consciousness transfer but experiencing it. Being the first independent witness. The fame, the recognition, everything I'd worked for...

"I need a minute to think." The words came out steadier than I felt.

Susan nodded. "Take some time."

"Can I go outside? It...might be my last chance."

One of the androids nodded, and Felix spoke from it. "I'll come with you."

My lungs burned on the stairs. The intensity with which the disease was spreading was almost unbelievable. No natural pathogen would attack this viciously and quickly, but if Vance's suspicions were correct, it was not from nature. I passed through the foyer and felt Shiva's mocking smile as I exited into the sun.

Gravel crunched under the android's feet as I crossed the

driveway to the pond and sat on the bench facing the water. The school of koi was catching bugs on the surface.

The journalist in me screamed this was insane. That I should run, expose the story, spread the uncertainty that I was starting to feel but couldn't articulate. Blow the whistle on what Felix was doing.

But that other part of me, the part he'd seen so clearly, couldn't stop imagining the possibilities. Being first. Being remembered. The story that would cement my legacy.

Even if I didn't fully believe everything Felix had said, I did believe my time was short. I could feel pieces of me being eaten away from the inside. If I were going to die anyway, I could at least have a death with meaning.

But was I really considering this? Abandoning my body, my physical existence, based on the word of a man who'd already deceived me? This wasn't a story I was chasing anymore. It was my life, my consciousness, my existence at stake.

I pulled out my phone, staring at the blank screen. Who would I even call? My editor would think I'd lost my mind. I had no wife or girlfriend. No siblings. I was estranged from my parents. The few friends I had would try to talk me out of it, drag me to a hospital. And maybe they'd be right. Maybe I should fight this the traditional way, even if my chances were slim.

The android sat down next to me, keeping a respectful distance. For several minutes, neither of us spoke. I watched the koi circle beneath the surface, their movements hypnotic, as I tried to quiet the storm in my mind.

"I'm sorry for not telling you." Felix's voice finally broke the silence, sounding softer through the android's speakers. I wondered what Susan might have said to him on the way up.

A harsh cough interrupted me. "I wouldn't have come." As I looked out on the pond again, it occurred to me that this seat must have been where Susan fell asleep on Felix before she died. "I can't forgive you, Felix."

"I know. I'm not asking you to." We sat in silence for a moment before he continued. "You said no more sales pitch… but Rohan, millions, perhaps billions, of people are going to feel the pain and fear you're feeling right now in the coming months and years."

I shook my head. "You can't know that."

"Vance was right. I've seen the data, all of it, and I spent the last few weeks looking for any alternative, and found nothing. If I had more time, maybe I could have found something. But the time to act is quickly running out. I know this was wrong… but maybe we can turn it into something good."

A pair of ducks floated along the surface of the pond. Rage still burned through me, but exhaustion was slowly winning. "What did it feel like?"

"Like waking up from a nap. Though without a hint of fatigue. I feel better in here than I did out there."

I snorted. "You're still selling."

"I can't help myself."

We sat in silence again. I tried to imagine leaving my body behind, existing only as data, as consciousness without flesh.

"How do you know you're really you?" I asked. "How do you know you're not just a copy that thinks it's Felix?"

The android shifted slightly. "I've been grappling with that too. But I remember everything. Not just facts but how things felt. The weight of exhaustion, the taste of coffee, the specific ache in my lower back from years of bad posture. If I'm a copy, I'm a perfect one. And if a perfect copy is indistinguishable from the original. Does the distinction matter?"

"Philosophy won't cure the plague," I muttered, but his words gnawed at me.

"No," he agreed. "But it might help you make peace with your choice."

A wave of dizziness passed through me as my decision crystallized. Felix was right. I wasn't ready to die. Not in two days, not in three. And as scary as climbing into that pod and transferring into Meru was, this sickness was scarier.

"I'm afraid," I rasped.

"I was too. Not just this time, but every time." He paused for a moment. "I tried to keep one thing in mind, though."

"What's that?"

"Our greatest work is just beyond our greatest fear."

Silence stretched between us. Felix's android sat quietly, no longer pushing, no longer selling. The choice was mine now, truly mine. And as I sat there, dying, I realized I'd already made it.

"I'll do it," I said, the words coming out stronger than I expected. "Not for you. For me."

The android nodded slowly, then held out a metallic hand, palm up, inviting me.

And I took it.

EPILOGUE

Vance arrived at Felix's house shortly after I transferred. Felix was right that my transfer was key in reconciling their relationship. I feel awful for what I did, for how I convinced Vance to be complicit in Felix's deception. But I didn't know. I couldn't have back then.

Felix got Imgen back, with Vance beside him at the helm. They brought the transfer technology to market just in time to help ease the incredible pain of the plague.

I was not alone in here for long. People arrived in trickles, then floods, thanks to my broadcasting of life inside "paradise." And by the time I discovered what had happened, it was too late to fix what I had done.

The signs were there, had I looked at them closer. I should have questioned Felix's sudden change in character more. Why he was so much darker after transferring. Why he was so quick to provide an explanation for what had happened to his body. I was so scared of dying that I stopped asking questions. I gave in to hope. To faith.

If you're reading this, Felix, I may have helped you build this world, but now I'm set on ending it. You bullied me into submission with your grand speeches about greatness. But rest assured, I will end Meru. I don't fear death anymore. What I fear is letting your world continue.

For anyone else reading this, spread this book however you can. Make copies. Share them. The key to ending Meru is in these pages, and if I fail, someone must carry the torch. If you find a way to get this in the hands of the few people remaining earthside, even better. We need their help. I don't think we can end Meru from within Meru.

Then find me. I can't tell you where to look, but I assure you, I'm still here. We all are. The people who've quietly gone missing over the years. Who saw through what Felix did and carved our refuge out of a part of his world where he can't reach us.

We're here. We're waiting. And we can wait a very long time.

BEFORE YOU GO

THANK YOU FOR READING *THE BIRTH OF PARADISE*!

This book is self-published, so if you enjoyed it, I would deeply appreciate any way you can help spread the word. Leaving a review on Amazon or Goodreads will help other people find it and would mean the world to me.

But the best thing you can do is to text a friend and suggest they read it. I'm sure you know one person who might enjoy exploring Felix's world as much as you have, and despite our world inching slower toward his vision by the day, word of mouth still drives the success of books more than anything else.

Finally, if you want to hear about the next book in the Meru Initiative when it launches, I encourage you to sign up for my newsletter at www.meruinitiative.com.

Thank you again for reading!

ACKNOWLEDGMENTS

AFTER FINISHING *HUSK*, I KNEW I WANTED TO SPEND more time in Felix's world. He's a fascinating character and I needed more of his backstory before diving into Husk's direct sequel. I wrote this book in a fit of inspiration over two months, working hard against the deadline of my third daughter being born and knowing I wanted to wrap it up before she arrived.

As such, fewer people touched it than any of my previous books. I rather liked it that way for this one; it felt as much for me as for anyone else. But special thanks must go first and foremost to my wife, Cosette, for her support as always throughout this writing journey and for reading drafts and giving me ever-useful feedback.

Thanks as well to my writing partner Nathan Baugh for the countless conversations and discussions about this book, the Meru Initiative, and writing in general. And thank you to my sister Sonja and dear friend Adil Majid for their helpful feedback.

Last, thank you as always to the team at Scribe: Rachael, David, Anna, Geoff, Caroline, and Eric, as well as Jeff with Lucent Audio, for turning this from a document file on my computer into a beautiful little novella.

www.ingramcontent.com/pod-product-compliance
Lightning Source LLC
Chambersburg PA
CBHW050153110726
47898CB00008B/2784